John Henry watched the forge glow bright with molten metal and sighed. He had wanted to stay away from weapons work. But sometimes it was necessary to fight fire with fire.

From the forge he drew a fearsome mask of glowing steel—a helmet that would protect his head and conceal the top half of his face.

He examined it carefully, then plunged it into a tub of icy water. It hissed and squeaked. When he lifted it out it was gleaming, stainless and cold.

Sparks and Uncle Joe stood nearby, watching. Joe nodded. "So . . . John Henry *Irons* has turned himself into *steel.*"

John Henry said, "I think now's the time for a little test."

Novelization by
LOUISE SIMONSON

Based on the screenplay written
by KENNETH JOHNSON

based upon characters published by DC Comics

STEEL created by LOUISE SIMONSON
and JON BOGDANOVE

Copyright © 1997 DC Comics. All Rights Reserved.

STEEL and all related characters, names, and indicia are trademarks of DC Comics © 1997. All Rights Reserved.

Published by Troll Communications L.L.C.

Printed in the United States of America.

10 9 8 7 6 5 4 3 2 1

First edition

For Jon Bogdanove and Mike Carlin,
without whom Steel wouldn't exist

ACKNOWLEDGMENTS
With admiration and thanks to
Jerry Siegel and Joe Shuster, creators of Superman;
to Chantal d'Aulnis, whose department
it is always a pleasure to work for;
and to Charles Kochman (thanks, Charlie!).

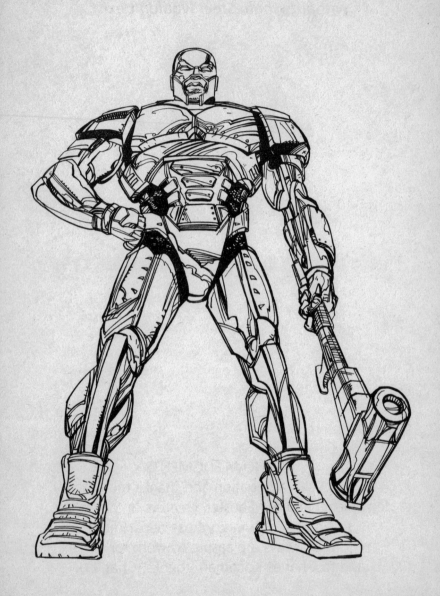

Amazing Weaponry

A towering soldier dressed in camouflage gear stood as still as the trees in the forest that surrounded him. He heard it first—the grinding of its ponderous treads as it crushed small trees in its path.

Then, the huge tank came lumbering over the rise, like an ancient predator. It paused. With chilling power it rotated its gun turret slowly, seeking its target, ready to fire.

With a practiced motion, the soldier swiftly lifted a high-tech rifle to his shoulder . . . and fired first.

A blast of roiling energy erupted from the barrel of the rifle and blew apart the tank's heavy treads. The tank's armored side began to glow red hot.

Suddenly the hatch popped open. A crewman leaped out, waving a white flag. "That's enough!" he shouted. "I surrender! It's an oven in there! My tail's on fire!"

The giant soldier laughed. "Thought I smelled some-thing roasting."

Beyond him in the forest, a camouflaged military team whooped and cheered. Their leader, Colonel Maxwell David, said what the others were feeling. "That, John Henry, is the sweet smell of victory."

Colonel David nodded to a sharp-eyed female soldier. Lieutenant Susan Sparks spoke into her walkie-talkie. "First weapons test terminated." Sparks flashed a grin at John Henry. "Nice shooting, Johnny."

John Henry Irons grinned down at her. Sparks may have come only to the middle of his chest, but her spirit was huge. And she was smart. She was as important to the team as he was.

"Thanks, Sparky," he said as he fingered the rifle's controls. "Moving the capacitors toward the stock really fixed the balance."

Sparks smiled modestly. "Always glad to help."

From behind them came a voice, "Of course, that was *my* idea!"

Sparks opened her mouth to protest, then shrugged. Nathaniel Burke, the third member of their weapons design team, always claimed credit. Particularly in front of Colonel David.

Today, however, Burke had a special reason for polishing his image. Senator Anne Nolan was visiting from the Senate Arms Appropriation Task Force. Burke wanted to impress her.

John Henry walked toward the shattered tank. Colonel David and the senator followed. As Sparks began to gather up her monitoring equipment, Burke crouched beside her, murmuring, "Stick with me, Sparks . . . there's no telling how far we'll go."

"Right now, I wouldn't go across the street with you," she said, shooting the man an angry look. She grabbed her gear and stalked toward the group studying the tank. Burke watched her with narrowed eyes.

"What's with Burke?" asked John Henry as the lieutenant stood beside him. "He looks mad enough to kill!"

Sparks shrugged. "Forget Burke." She changed the subject. "How's the voltage holding?"

"Solid," John Henry assured her. "Check the amp curve. It's—"

"Perfect!" She pushed a button and smiled as a series of glowing green numbers interpreted every aspect of the rifle's performance. "Stats on the rifle's LED readout verify it. Your new alloy kept the barrel cool."

John pointed a finger at her. "Cool, just like you."

Sparks smiled and pointed back. The tips of their fingers touched. It was a ritual they'd started when they became teammates.

Burke watched them, scowling. He didn't want to be a member of their cozy little club. He had more important fish to fry. He smoothed his expression and walked over to the senator. "Impressed, ma'am?" he asked.

"It's amazing weaponry," she said, sincerely. "Was the rifle fired at maximum power?"

Burke smiled. "Irons and Sparks have taken it as far as they can. But I've personally made some adjustments to a second prototype that ups the intensity considerably."

The senator's eyes glinted. "That would be something

to see, Lieutenant Burke," she said. "Keep that up and you'll make captain in no time."

As Colonel David suggested that they move on, John Henry and Sparks walked ahead to set up their second demonstration. Burke glanced contemptuously at his teammates. They might be willing to share the glory, he thought, but he wasn't. He didn't want to drudge away forever in some cluttered army workshop. He planned to be in charge—and not down the road. Sometime soon. Very soon.

Pushing the Envelope

Senator Nolan and Colonel David followed John Henry and the others down the main street of a deserted adobe village, filled with bombed-out-looking buildings.

The village had been set up as a training area, Colonel David explained. They would stage the demonstration from the old church in the town square.

The senator and colonel watched from the back of the church as John Henry muscled a sleek electronic cannon into a window and aimed it at a wall across the street. "That man is one big guy," the senator said. "He should've been NBA."

"Said he never had the knack for basketball," Colonel David told her. "He joined up at seventeen after his parents died. The army sent him to college. He discovered he had a real gift for metallurgy."

The senator smiled. "He's got the right name for it. Irons, isn't it?"

"Right. John Henry Irons. He developed high-grade alloys for these weapons and some incredible armor plating. Sparks is our electronics specialist. They're good team players."

"And Burke?" the senator asked.

"A loner," the colonel answered heartily. "But a genius. Loves creating these powerful, high-tech toys. He's always pushing the envelope."

The senator moved closer to study the weapon. Sparks looked up from tightening a bolt. "The sonic cannon pumps out an ultra-low frequency burst of sound-energy. It can take out a whole line of troops—"

John Henry picked up the thought. "Without killing them. Just leaves them stunned."

The senator was amused. "And you like that idea. Odd for a soldier, isn't it?"

John Henry grinned. "Not killing? Maybe, ma'am, but, yeah, I like it!"

"Set to a higher gain, the cannon can bring down a wall," Sparks explained. "That's what we'll be demonstrating."

Burke came in, brushing the dust from his hands. Dramatically, he whispered, "Just the wall? Why not the whole building?"

Sparks scowled. "Forget it, Burke! We haven't tested those parameters."

No time like the present, Burke thought to himself. As John Henry moved to man the weapon, Burke grinned engagingly. "May I do the honors, Colonel?" he asked.

Colonel David nodded. John Henry surrendered the firing position. "Go for it, Burke," the colonel ordered.

Burke caught the senator's eye. He glanced down at the cannon meaningfully. The senator nodded her understanding. As the senator watched, Burke slid his fingers along the barrel, feeling for the control. Silently, he turned it all the way to the maximum.

John Henry caught the motion out of the corner of his eye. Realizing the danger, he dove desperately toward Burke, shouting for him to stop. But even as he tackled Burke aside, he heard the loud *ka-vvoom!* and realized he was too late.

A shock wave of thunderous sound roared across the dusty street and slammed into the target building. In an instant, its walls imploded violently.

Then, as John Henry and the others watched in helpless horror, the rumbling shock wave bounced back toward the church in which they were waiting.

The walls collapsed around them. Burke, John Henry, and the colonel were thrown back by the blast. Behind them, John Henry heard the crash of concrete and the startled cries of Sparks and the senator.

John looked around frantically, calling, "Sparks! Sparky!?" But there was no answer.

He leaped over Burke's bloodied, unconscious body. The colonel staggered to his knees, stunned. "Burke . . . what in heaven's name did he do?"

John Henry couldn't spare the breath to answer. Desperately, he stumbled over to where Sparks and the senator had been standing.

He grabbed the ragged edge of a heavy concrete slab. With all his massive strength, he struggled to lift it. Just when it seemed his veins would burst, the slab finally moved.

Beneath it lay the two women's crushed, torn bodies.

Court Martial

"Lieutenant Irons, when you managed to move the concrete, what did you find?" the prosecuting major asked John Henry.

John sat in the witness chair beside the judge's bench. He scanned the courtroom.

Burke sat at the defense table, neatly dressed in his lieutenant's uniform. He leaned across to whisper to his defense attorney, and John Henry saw the ugly scar that marred his temple. Burke refused to meet John Henry's eyes.

"The senator was dead, sir," John Henry said grimly.

"And Lieutenant Sparks?" the prosecutor asked.

John Henry remembered how Sparks had lain, bloody and dazed, amid the rubble. "Her legs were crushed," he said. "She has a spinal injury and might not walk again, sir."

The prosecutor said, "We've heard testimony that you tried to stop Lieutenant Burke from firing. Did you see how the weapon was calibrated? What intensity level was set?"

"The maximum, sir," John Henry answered.

"A parameter that had never been tested or even approved for testing, is that correct?" the prosecutor pressed.

John Henry looked directly at Burke. His eyes blazed as he answered. "Yes, sir. I saw Burke deliberately recalibrate the weapon. He knew what he was doing."

"Thank you, Lieutenant Irons," the prosecutor said gravely. "That will be all."

As John Henry walked away from the courtroom down a deserted corridor, Burke called out angrily, "Thanks for selling me out, brother soldier."

John Henry growled, "You'll pay for what you did to Sparks, Burke!"

Burke snarled at John Henry, barely able to contain his fury. "Pay? Do you know what I could have done with military resources behind me? Do you know where I was headed?"

John Henry turned his back on him. In a voice filled with contempt, he said, "I know where you're headed now."

The court martial was over and the verdict rendered.

Outside the military court building, Colonel David told John Henry that he'd done the right thing in testifying against Burke. "He's lucky he was only discharged and not sent to prison," Colonel David said sadly. "Sure hate to lose him, though. He is one brilliant guy."

John Henry glanced at the colonel sharply. "I doubt if Sparks feels the same way."

Colonel David sighed. "Well, it's been a rotten deal all around, but you'll feel better as soon as we get back to work. We've got to assemble a new unit and press on. We've got a golden opportunity here."

John Henry stared at the colonel, not believing what he was hearing. "What do you mean, opportunity?" he asked.

The colonel raked his fingers through his hair as he tried to explain. "Look, John, nobody's sorrier than me that people got hurt. But that's the nature of war."

"But we're not *at* war, sir," John Henry said grimly. "I thought the whole idea of these weapons was to stop an enemy *without* hurting them."

Colonel David sighed. "I know that's why you like them." Then he continued with growing enthusiasm. "But, John, these weapons are more powerful than I ever hoped. You saw how those buildings folded. We've created the next generation of weaponry. We can't turn our backs on that kind of potential firepower!"

John Henry's eyes flashed. "Maybe *you* can't. But after what happened to Sparks, *I* can, sir." He saluted the flabbergasted Colonel David and walked away.

From the shadows of the courthouse wall, Nathaniel Burke watched with hatred in his eyes. Burke knew what he was going to do—how he was going to get rich, *and* even. Leaning lazily against the side of the courthouse, he plotted his revenge, a cruel grin on his lips.

Looking Forward

John Henry walked down the hall of the military hospital past the nurses' station of the Intensive Care Unit. A frequent visitor, he was waved past.

Stopping outside Sparks's room, he peered in. She lay on her bed, wrapped like a mummy in casts and bandages. Tubes and wires ran from her body, connecting her to machines that beeped and flashed. Her eyes were swollen almost shut.

But when John Henry stepped into the room, she smiled. "My hero," she said softly.

John held up the bouquet of sweet peas he'd brought for her. "My favorite," she whispered.

"No kidding? Really?" John hadn't known she especially liked the delicate flowers.

"Not just the flowers," Sparks whispered. "You." She

weakly pointed her finger at John. Responding to their ritual, he touched her fingertip with his own.

Then she noticed he was wearing jeans. "You really did bail, huh?" she asked.

John Henry nodded sadly. "After what happened to you, I can't go back."

"I'll come see you . . . soon as I'm back on my feet," Sparks croaked.

John Henry nodded, even though he knew—everybody knew—she'd probably never walk again. "I'm looking forward to that. And I'm going to be checking up on you every week."

"Where are you heading?" Sparks asked, fighting back tears. She was going to miss him terribly.

"Home," John Henry said. "To my family in L.A."

Razzle-Dazzle

Learning John Henry's destination was child's play, Burke thought as he settled comfortably into his first-class seat on a westbound jet. Johnny was going home to his grandma and little brother.

He sneered. What Burke had waiting for him in L.A. was far more important than family. He had contacts. And plans!

The former lieutenant ran his fingers over his scar. When his plans were implemented, he would have it all—wealth and power. But best of all, he would have revenge.

———

As Burke had arranged, the airport car rental agency had a convertible waiting for him in L.A. He smiled with satisfaction as he tossed his suitcase into the the sports car's small trunk. He checked the breast pocket of his jacket to make sure the floppy disk was still there.

Then he drove his rental car out through the city and along the Pacific Coast Highway toward Santa Monica.

He parked outside a modest five-story office building with a huge neon sign that flashed the name: DANTASTIC.

With confidence, he strode through swinging doors into a lobby that buzzed and flashed with high-tech arcade video games and pinball machines.

Burke walked past buyers examining the razzle-dazzle units to the receptionist's desk and asked to see Mr. Daniels.

"How're you doing, Big Willy?" Burke said as he entered the luxurious fifth-floor corner office of Willy Daniels. He hardly glanced at the wraparound windows with their panoramic view of the Pacific Ocean. Burke had eyes only for the small man in the expensive, custom-made suit who swiveled in his chair to face him.

"Nice setup you got here," Burke continued. "You've come a long way from the old neighborhood. But word on the street is you're still dealing hot weapons."

Daniels stared at Burke, his eyes icy. Behind him stood two impassive lieutenants, a sinewy blonde woman named Duvray and a powerfully built man named Singer.

"I distribute arcade games," Daniels said coldly as he chewed on a mint-flavored toothpick. "I also belong to the Chamber of Commerce. And I give jobs to a lot of at-risk kids. I don't know what you've heard, but—"

Burke grinned. "I've heard you'll still sell your mother for a roll of quarters."

Duvray and Singer stiffened, but Daniels stopped them with a gesture. "You come here to get your butt kicked, Burke?" he asked.

Burke leaned confidently on Daniels's desk. "Is that any way to talk to a man who's going to make you *really* big, Willy?" he asked. "How'd you like to deal the next generation of superweapons . . . not to the crooks and punks on the street, but to the world?"

Daniels raised his eyebrows. He was beginning to be interested.

"Give me some seed money to build the prototypes and do a little advertising," Burke continued. "We'll be partners."

Daniels looked at him speculatively. "You were with the army, weren't you? What exactly are you selling?" he asked.

Burke pulled out the floppy disk. "Oh, now—*that's* top secret."

Good to Be Home

John Henry took the bus home. As it rumbled into Los Angeles, he reflected on his life and what to do with it. He smiled. Eventually, he'd figure out the big picture, but right now, he just wanted to get home.

He swung off the city bus at Ingram Street, near his old neighborhood. His grandmother and brother knew he was coming, but he hadn't told them when he would arrive. He was planning to surprise them.

He turned onto Witmer. As he passed a little girl skipping rope, he grinned. A basketball rolled into his path and he picked it up. Some kids playing ball on a beat-up neighborhood court yelled, "Go for it!"

John Henry aimed, then shot. The ball arced through the air and bounded off the bare hoop. The kids laughed and John Henry grinned and shrugged. Big as I am, he thought, I'd never make it in the NBA.

Suddenly, from behind, a voice shouted, "In-com-ing!"

John Henry turned as his thirteen-year-old brother, Martin, streaked right at him on a skateboard. With the grace of a bullfighter, John pirouetted aside and scooped the boy up.

"You'll get hurt like that, rocketing in here like some kind of Scud missile!" John Henry said.

Martin laughed as his brother swung him back to the ground. "'Scud'?—you mean stud!" He flipped his skateboard up to his hand. He was excited to see his brother, but he was in public and trying to be cool.

Lamont, a tough-looking kid, passed. "What's up, Martin?" Lamont asked.

"Peace," Martin answered. Martin and Lamont popped fists.

"Lamont's brother still in jail?" John Henry said when Lamont was out of earshot.

"Man, his brother got more time than a clock," Martin said.

"And you're hanging with Lamont?" John Henry asked sternly.

Martin held up his hands defensively. "Hey, back off. I ain't living like that. What you think?"

John Henry looked at Martin carefully. "I think it's good to be home," he said.

Martin burst through the front door of his grandmother's brownstone. "Grandma Odessa! Guess what?" he shouted.

Grandma Odessa bustled out of her kitchen, flapping her hands frantically. "Shhhh! Hush your mouth, Martin, before you ruin everything," she whispered.

"Sorry," Martin whispered back. But he couldn't hide his broad grin. "Somebody's here to see you."

John Henry stuck his head around the door. "Hey, Grandma!" he shouted.

"Shhhhhh!" Odessa shushed him. She tiptoed to the door and threw her arms around him. "Oh Lord, how I've missed you, son," she said softly.

John Henry hugged her back. "I've missed you, too, G. O.," he said. "What's up?"

Grandma Odessa led her grandsons into the kitchen. Cookbooks were piled on tables and spilling off chairs. John Henry had never seen so many cookbooks in his life.

As she peered gingerly into the oven, she gave a frustrated sigh. Using a potholder, she pulled out a casserole dish. A flat brown mass lay inside. "It was *supposed* to be a hominy souffle," she explained in a normal voice.

"A souffle?" John Henry asked.

"It's supposed to be all light and fluffy and full of air," Grandma Odessa said. "And it *was* until you two came storming in. Martin, how am I ever going to master the art of French cooking when you keep crashing in here like James Brown screaming, 'I feel good!'"

John Henry raised a quizzical eyebrow.

"I'm marrying my down-home recipes with French cooking," she explained.

Martin grinned proudly. "She wants to open a restaurant and call it Black and Bleu."

John Henry started to laugh. Then he looked at his grandmother. Realizing her seriousness, he decided to smile instead. "Well, that's a . . . cool name," he said.

Odessa told Martin to do his homework while his brother unpacked. "I don't want more of those notes from your teachers," she said sternly.

Martin ran upstairs to hit the books. Maybe, if he hurried, he could talk his brother into shooting baskets with him later. He always enjoyed it, even though his seven-foot-tall brother was terrible at basketball.

John looked after him with a worried frown. "The gangs still trying to recruit him?" he asked.

Odessa sighed. "Worse than ever. It's hard to keep him straight. I'm glad you're back. Now go unpack. There's a batch of phone messages on your bed—job offers. From weapons makers. Is that why you left the service?" she asked. "To make more money?"

John Henry stood straighter. "No. No more weapons. It's lots better for my soul."

Grandma Odessa hugged him close. "I love you, John Henry. And I'm behind you, whatever you choose to do. But I want you to know I like this decision just fine," she said proudly.

John Henry smiled down into her eyes. "I love you, too, Grandma," he said.

Crowley Metals didn't make weapons—it made industrial metals. John Henry smiled lazily as he stirred a cauldron of molten steel. The job was undemanding, but for now that was just what he wanted.

When the whistle blew for lunch, he handed over his paddle and wiped his face with a towel. Then he walked over to a pay phone and started pumping in quarters.

A young secretary smiled flirtatiously at John Henry as she came around to hand him his paycheck. John Henry politely nodded his thanks, then continued speaking into the phone. "This is the VA hospital in Oklahoma City, right? But I know Lieutenant Susan Sparks is in rehab there. I've talked to her. Transferred to St. Louis? Yeah, give me the address."

John Henry scribbled the address on the back of his paycheck envelope and sighed. If Sparks was in St. Louis, it meant the doctors in Oklahoma City felt they had done all they could for her there.

It had been three months since the accident, and every time he talked to her she sounded more hopeless. Like her life was over. Like she was beginning to believe she would never be of any use again.

He knew that wasn't true. He just didn't know yet how to convince Sparks of it.

Research and Development

In a secret subbasement beneath Dantastic, Big Willy Daniels and his lieutenants Duvray and Singer walked past hard-eyed workers packing AK-47s in arcade game shipping crates.

This was Daniels's distribution warehouse for illegal weaponry—the *real* source of his wealth.

In an open area they watched as Burke hefted a high-tech rifle.

"As promised, Daniels, here's the prototype. Want to see how she performs?" Burke handed the rifle to an assistant.

As they stepped back to watch the fireworks, Daniels glanced at Burke. "The front office said there's a kid you want to hire."

Burke smiled. "Just a little personal score to settle.

Giving back to the community, so to speak."

The assistant raised the rifle and aimed it at a human-shaped target set up at the end of a shadowy hall. On Burke's command, he pulled the trigger.

A burst of roiling energy rocketed out of the muzzle. Simultaneously, a flash exploded out of the breechblock, hitting the assistant full in the face.

The assistant dropped the rifle and grabbed his eyes, screaming in pain. Duvray rushed to his side. "Get him upstairs and call 911! Tell them it was an electrical fire," she said.

As several workers rushed to help, Duvray turned on Burke angrily. "What are you going to do about this?" she asked.

Burke calmly picked up the rifle and studied it. "I'm going to adjust the surge protector," he said.

His lack of concern for his assistant infuriated Duvray. "You nearly killed that man," she said. "You could have killed us all!"

Burke looked at her, his eyes as lethal as the rifle he held. "I had to push the envelope," he said.

Duvray snarled. "Mr. Daniels, this guy's a nutcase."

"Duvray, look at the target," Daniels said calmly.

The blonde woman started to argue, then glanced hotly toward the target. It was shredded.

Daniels chewed on his toothpick. "Good job, Burke. Keep up the fine work," he said.

Duvray left her fifth-floor office and walked to the elevator, glad she had brought her umbrella to work. It looked like rain.

In the upper lobby, she nodded to Singer, who was waiting for the elevator. Burke walked up and smiled at Duvray. She glared at him.

The elevator door slid open and Duvray and Singer stepped inside. Burke started to follow, then paused. "Darn! I forgot something. Hey, Singer, give me a hand, will you?"

Singer shrugged and stepped out past Duvray. As the elevator doors closed, Duvray's eyes met Burke's. He smiled his cobra smile and waved good-bye.

Duvray didn't like the smile or what it promised. She reached out to block the doors from closing, but it was too late. They sealed shut with a hiss and the elevator started to descend.

Outside the elevator, in the lobby, Singer watched Burke pull a small remote control device from his pocket and press a button.

Suddenly, the circuit box above the elevator exploded in a series of high-voltage flashes. Heavy metal wrenched and the elevator cable motor spun wildly out of control.

The elevator plummeted into the sub-subbasement. Singer heard Duvray's scream of terror end in a horrific crash.

Singer stared at Burke, stunned, wondering why he had been spared. Burke gently took his arm. "I need someone to work closely with me, someone I can trust," Burke explained. "Is that you?"

Two months later, under the direct command of Nathaniel Burke, Singer's new recruits were ready to go out for Big Willy Daniels and loyally conquer new worlds.

Firepower

Officer Norma Johnson drove her squad car westbound along Fourth Street. John Henry was wedged into the front seat across from her. Norma and John Henry had been good friends since grade school. She was glad to have him back in the neighborhood.

Crammed between them, Martin folded his arms and slouched. "What's with this 'town meeting' stuff? It sounds whack," he grumbled.

Norma smiled. "It could help get the new antigang program set up. I thought you two might be able to share some insights." She glanced pointedly at Martin. "You might even learn something."

Martin slouched down even farther in his seat. "Why learn when I can earn?" he complained. "One of my friends wants me to work at a place called Dantastic. They sell arcade games. They're the best!"

John Henry grinned. "Now that's just what I'm talking about. Get into something legit."

Martin sat forward hopefully. "So that means I don't have to go to this meeting, right?"

"Wrong!" John Henry and Norma sang out.

Martin slumped as John Henry and Norma traded amused smiles.

Two blocks away, Singer sat behind the steering wheel of a sleek armored Humvee. The gray metal vehicle, built like a small tank, prowled to a corner beside an automated bank teller. Its motor rumbled angrily.

Singer glanced over his shoulder. "It's time to make our CompuBank withdrawal," he growled.

A small sideport on the Humvee hissed open, revealing the muzzle of a large cannon pointed at the bank's front window. The cannon fired an ultralow-frequency sonic burst, and the window and wall exploded.

The Humvee beamed a high-intensity laser through the demolished window-wall, carving effortlessly into the metal vault. Five men in black hoods leaped from the vehicle, dove into the bank, and began grabbing up bags of money.

Inside Norma's squad car, the police radio squawked out a warning. "All units in the vicinity: possible two-one-one in progress, two-two-one-eight Sixth Street."

"A robbery," Norma said as she snatched up her mike. "Three-Adam-six. I'm on it. Request backup."

Norma hit her siren. Martin's eyes lit up like the car's now-whirling flashers. "Yeah!" he said. "Let's get ready to rumble!"

At the end of the street, Norma spotted four hooded men emerging from the destroyed bank lobby, lugging heavy bags and hooting with delight. Suddenly, another squad car roared past Norma's. It screeched to a halt and two cops bailed out, their guns drawn.

As Norma and John Henry watched, the thieves unslung high-tech rifles from their shoulders and opened fire. Roiling energy blasted from the muzzles, hitting the cops and blowing them backward.

John Henry felt a growing horror. He knew those weapons.

Ordering Martin to stay down, he slid from the squad car and ran to help the fallen cops. Ignoring him, Martin followed.

Norma shouted into her radio, "Officers down! We have a problem here!"

She saw the thieves piling into the van. "They're going to get clean away," she muttered softly to herself. Then she realized there was still one way she could stop them.

From behind the wheel of the Humvee, Singer watched the squad car drive into the center of the road and block his path. "Bad move, sugar," he snarled.

The cannon swiveled. *Ka-voom!* A tidal wave of low-frequency sound slammed against Norma's two-thousand-pound police car, flipping it over like a Hot Wheels toy.

Kneeling beside the downed officers, John Henry and Martin watched, horrified, as the sound wave rolled on, shearing off a fire hydrant and slamming the squad car upside down against a building. The engine burst into flames.

John Henry dashed toward the burning squad car. Desperately he squinted through the shattered windshield. Inside, Norma was unconscious. He kicked in a side window and managed to haul her free just as the squad car exploded in a burst of searing heat and shredding metal.

Kneeling beside Norma, he felt for a pulse. She was alive but badly injured. John Henry asked himself again what kind of firepower the thieves had used, but he was afraid his suspicions were right.

He looked up as the Humvee rumbled past him into the night.

Where's Cutter?

As the Humvee turned off Sixth Street, Singer glanced in the rearview mirror. He could still see flame-lit smoke rising to stain the L.A. night sky. He grinned. Three cops down, a bank vault emptied, a squad car burning like a bonfire, and a clean getaway—all in less than three minutes. This sure beat working as a bodyguard.

Singer called back to the gang members, who were popping fists and hooting with excitement. "Hey, Slats, everybody accounted for?"

Slats, the leader of the thieves, pulled off his mask, revealing the patch that covered his left eye and gave him his street name. He glanced around the truck. "Hey! Cutter's not here!"

As John Henry stared after the Humvee, Martin yelled, "Somebody's still in the bank!"

Cutter's head jerked up as he heard the shout. He looked around wildly, then sprinted from the ruined vault, stuffing money into his pockets as he ran out.

"Martin, look out for Norma until I get back," John Henry growled as he leaped after the thief.

Cutter scrambled down a hillside, ducked beneath a freeway underpass, and sprinted past a group of homeless men huddled around a fiery oil drum.

For an instant, dazzled by the glow from the fire, John Henry lost the man. Then he saw him run down an alley.

Cutter clambered over a fence and raced away, pulling off his hood as he ran. Something was slung over his shoulder. To John Henry, it looked ominously like the pulse rifle he had invented.

John Henry vaulted over the fence, gathering steam like a locomotive as he ran. Cutter glanced back, worried. He scrambled beneath some tractor trailers, then over a fence into a railroad yard.

A lineman grabbed Cutter, shouting, "Hey, we're switching! You'll get killed here!"

Cutter hit the lineman hard, sending him flying backward down an embankment and onto the tracks, unconscious.

John Henry pulled the lineman to safety, seconds before the wheels of a ninety-ton hopper car rolled over the tracks where his head had been.

Leaving the man in the care of his colleagues, John Henry dashed after Cutter.

Cutter zipped past a beefy steel coupler. John Henry

followed, closer now. By the lights of the switching yard, he could see the thief's purple bandanna flapping as he ran.

Cutter dodged around a rolling forty-ton tank car and leaped across the tracks just ahead of a diesel pulling a freight train. Creaking and rumbling, it blocked John Henry's path.

John Henry was determined not to let the man get away. He grabbed the handhold of a gondola car. Straining, he pulled himself up, clambered across the jostling couple, then jumped off on the other side.

The thief was nowhere to be seen.

Cutter crouched behind a parked railroad car, gasping for breath. Peering out from behind a wheel, he watched the large man who was pursuing him scan the area. Cutter grinned as he unslung the pulse rifle, aimed, and fired.

A blast of energy roared past John Henry's head and smacked against the edge of a railroad car. It splintered, and John Henry was spun back from the electrical impact. He landed with his back against the coupler.

He shook his head to clear it and looked up to see a huge boxcar rolling in with the iron mouth of its coupler open.

John Henry dove to the side just as the couples rammed together with a thunderous *klang*. He lay on his side, panting.

Cutter peered out from beneath the railroad car. His pursuer was still alive. But he wouldn't be for long. Cutter adjusted the rifle control and fired again.

A blast of low-frequency sound rammed the side of the boxcar. The car began to tip over—right on top of John Henry.

As it fell toward him like a wall, he knew he had one chance to survive.

Instinctively, John Henry swiftly rolled toward the spot where the boxcar's open side door could come down around him.

Cutter watched the boxcar smash onto its side. It lay there like a fallen dinosaur. He raised his fist in victory. That dude was tough, the teenager thought, but now he was history.

Cutter smirked as he climbed to his feet and sprinted toward the railroad yard exit.

Behind Cutter, the other side door of the boxcar slowly rolled open, and John Henry climbed out.

He saw the thief running toward the exit and took off after him. He eyed the rifle with respect. This time, he would approach more cautiously.

Cutter had almost reached the exit when he was slammed against the side of a Dumpster. The rifle was snatched from his hand.

At first, John Henry hardly noticed the gang member he held by a purple kerchief. He had eyes only for the rifle.

It was what he knew it would be. What he didn't want to believe was possible. It was one of the top-secret weapons he himself had helped create for the government.

John Henry tore his eyes from the rifle and focused them on the thief. "Where did you get this?" he growled.

Cutter stammered. "I—I found it!"

John Henry pulled him closer. "If you don't tell me where you 'found' it, you're going to find my fist in your mouth!"

Suddenly a blast of energy slammed into John Henry's back, blowing him forward, slamming him into a gutter. He lay there, stunned, unable to move, or even to breathe.

The hooded figure who had fired the rifle hauled Cutter to his feet. "C'mon!" he said. "We gotta get out of here!"

John Henry heard the staccato slap of their feet as they ran off into the darkness. He tried to rise, then slumped back onto the ground.

On the Mark

John Henry leaned against a battered neighborhood phone booth, snarling into the telephone. "What did I say to the police? What could I say? I know those weapons are top secret, Colonel David. I just want to know how they hit the streets!"

"The NSA says every rifle created for us is accounted for," Colonel David assured him. "There's no way highly classified weapons could have ended up in the hands of a street gang."

John Henry rubbed his bandaged neck and prayed for patience. "I had one in my hand, sir! What do you think blew over that squad car, a twister? I caught a gang kid holding a USR model 3.5 sonic—"

The colonel's panicked voice interrupted him. "John— are you calling from a secure phone?"

John Henry had heard enough. "What difference does that make now, sir? We have to do something about those weapons! And if you can't . . . or won't . . . then I will—sir!"

He slammed down the phone so furiously that the whole unit was knocked off the wall. As he stalked away he realized that he would have to get to the bottom of this himself. And the first step would be to find the gang that wore purple.

John Henry and his brother, Martin, sat on the steps of their brownstone. John Henry described the thief he had tangled with.

"Purple?" Martin started to speak, then bit his lip instead.

John Henry's eyes burned with frustration. "This isn't a joke, man! Who're you protecting?"

"You!" Martin growled. "I'm protecting you! Purple is the Marks. Those kids are buck wild!"

The Marks, John Henry thought. The Marks had his guns. "Where do they hang out?" he asked quietly.

Martin sighed. He hoped his brother wasn't going to do something stupid. "Back room at Benny's Pool Hall," he said.

In his mind, John Henry saw the Marks fire the guns he'd helped invent. He saw Norma hurt. He saw the bank destroyed. "Believe me, Martin, those Marks are going to hang," he said.

Benny's Pool Hall and "social club" was busy that afternoon. Teenaged gang members, wearing purple, shot pool and cheered as the TV news showed security camera views of the CompuBank robbery.

"As yet the police have no clues leading to the perpetrators of this amazing, high-tech robbery," the announcer said. The gang members hooted and popped fists.

Then John Henry stepped into the room, and it grew very quiet.

Slats, the leader of the Marks, stepped forward. "Yo! Check out the Jolly Black Giant," he joked.

The others chuckled as they moved casually to strategic positions around the room, surrounding John Henry. He stood firm, however, barely controlling his rage. "The guns you had. I want to know where you got the weapons."

Slats laughed. "What guns? Heard those heaters were awesome, though. Like to get me one."

Holdecker, his lieutenant, chortled. "I hear that, man."

John Henry looked at the gang leader with contempt.

"I thought you were in charge here," he said. "I see now you're just fronting for someone else."

Holdecker made a face and pretended to shudder. "And he's gonna pay, too! Ooh, I'm shaking like a leaf!" The other teenagers laughed.

John Henry jerked Holdecker off the floor. "Tell me what I want to know!" he snarled.

The gang reacted instantly. A dozen guns and knives were at John Henry's throat and head.

"Get out," Slats said. "We don't know nothing about those guns. But we know you. Don't come around here no more!"

John Henry glared at Slats and the gang. He dropped Holdecker and turned to leave. "You're going to know me a lot better," he said searingly. Then he stalked out the door.

When he was gone, Slats sauntered to the pay phone in the corner and called Nathaniel Burke.

Slats's call interrupted a meeting between Burke, Singer, and Big Willy Daniels. Slats told him John Henry had come into Benny's, just as Burke had predicted.

"All right," Burke said. "Nothing changes. Just keep your dumb friend Cutter out of sight!" He slammed down the phone and turned to Singer.

"Get rid of Cutter!" Burke ordered. "I have to set an example—I don't want others getting out of line."

Resuming their meeting, Burke asked Daniels, "Got the new Web page ready?"

Daniels nodded. "Be on-line in a week. We'll be wired for the world!"

"What about Irons?" Singer asked.

"We're covered," Burke said. "There's not a thing he can do."

Adding an Element

Where's this sculpture going?" John Henry asked his uncle Joe. Joe was an artist, a vital man in his late sixties.

"To Walker Museum in Minneapolis," Joe replied, using an acetylene torch to mold a piece of scrap metal into an abstract design. "They give me a commission. Hey, if they want to say it's art, I ain't gonna argue."

Joe's golden retriever, Lillie, yawned.

"It pays good," Uncle Joe continued. "I've made ten times more since I retired than I did in thirty years at the steel mill."

Usually John Henry liked to talk to Joe about the clever art he created from the odds and ends found in his junkyard "studio." But today he paced restlessly as Joe worked.

"What's the matter, boy?" Joe asked.

John Henry scowled as he sagged onto the seat of an old motorcycle. "I don't know how to fight back, Uncle Joe. I have to find out who put those weapons out on the street. I feel responsible. I helped create them!"

Uncle Joe kept cutting. "What you know about old Al Nobel?" he asked.

"Nobel? Like in the Nobel Peace Prize?" John asked.

"You know where that prize money comes from?" Uncle Joe asked. "Old Al Nobel come up with something he thought was going to be great for mankind. Called it tri-nitro-tol-u-een—TNT. Then he spent the rest of his life regretting it."

John Henry understood that. "He felt responsible."

"For all the people who died because of it. So Nobel established prizes for folks who work to make the world a better place."

John Henry looked up impatiently. "What're you trying to tell me, Uncle Joe?" he asked.

"I'm not trying to *tell* you anything. I'm just saying everybody ought to do their best. If working in a metal shop's the best a man can do, then he should do it well. And if a man's got skills for a higher calling, he better use them."

John Henry frowned. "What kind of 'skills' are you talking about? I'd have to be made of steel to take on all that firepower out on the street. Even the police don't have a chance."

"Maybe the police ain't enough. Maybe we need some new kind of firepower ourselves," Uncle Joe said.

"I told myself when I left the army that I was done with those weapons," John Henry said slowly. "And even if I had some, they're top secret. We'd get busted before we got started."

Uncle Joe glanced at John Henry. "They can only get you if they know who you are."

John Henry sighed. "But my specialty is metal."

"Yeah. And if I was going to make one of them alloys to make metal stronger, exactly what would I do?"

John Henry glanced up, puzzled. "Well, you'd add something to it. You'd have to add another element."

Uncle Joe grinned at John Henry. "Oh. Is *that* what you do?"

John Henry looked up into Uncle Joe's cagey eyes. Finally he understood what the old man was getting at.

The VA hospital in St. Louis was squat and gray and ugly. Seeing it, John Henry knew he should have come sooner.

He found Sparks in the recreation room, sitting in a wheelchair, staring dully out a dirty window. He walked up behind her. "Man, I thought my tax dollars went to keep these windows clean. How you doing, Sparky?"

"Great," Sparks muttered, but she didn't turn around. Even when he pointed his finger at her, awaiting their ritual, she just stared straight ahead.

In place of her once-bright eyes was a shadowy, tight mask of bitterness.

She looks like a zombie, John Henry thought. He sat slowly beside her. "Why'd you stop writing? Didn't you get my letters?"

"I got them," Sparks said dully. "And this wheelchair you ordered. Thanks."

John Henry tried again. "It must be hard on you. I can imagine how you feel."

Sparks chuckled darkly. "I don't think so," she said.

At least it was a real response, John Henry told himself. "You're right," he said. "I wish I could turn back the clock."

Sparks wheeled around to face him at last. "Sometimes you don't get a choice about things. Stuff happens." She was looking at John now, trying to keep up her veneer of tough sarcasm.

"Yeah, I know," he said. "A cop friend of mine just got hurt bad. With one of our weapons. They're on the streets."

"On the streets?" Sparks was fully alert now, and troubled. "How is that possible?"

He sighed. "That's what I'm trying to find out. I sure could use your help."

Sparks tapped her legs angrily. "Oh, yeah. I'd be a big help on the streets."

Now John Henry was getting angry, too. "What are you going to do, just sit here and stare out that dirty window forever?"

John Henry stood and moved toward the window, which had been painted shut years ago. He wrenched it open and paint chips went flying. A breeze fondled Sparks's hair. She stared outside, tears welling. "You want to know the truth, Johnny? I just want to die," she whispered.

John Henry started to turn her wheelchair. "You're talking crazy now! Come on, we're getting out of here!"

"What're you doing? No!" She clamped on the wheel brakes. That made John Henry smile. He liked her stubbornness. Not that it meant she was going to win. He scooped her up, wheelchair and all.

"Stop it! Irons, I don't want to go!" she shrieked.

John Henry laughed. For better or worse, his old, bossy Sparks was back. "Sorry, Sparks, sometimes you don't get a choice about things," he told her.

He carried her out of the rec room, through the hospital's gray corridors, and into the sunshine.

Not Your
Average Junkyard

Later that day, John Henry wheeled the still-disgruntled Sparks into Uncle Joe's junkyard.

Sparks wrinkled her nose. "And I thought the hospital was funky," she said. Joe's golden retriever loped over and licked her hand. Sparks actually smiled.

"That's Lillie," John Henry told her.

"Not your average junkyard dog," Sparks said, stroking Lillie's soft head.

John Henry grinned. "This isn't your average junkyard."

He wheeled her past Uncle Joe's amazing sculptures, toward a large geodesic dome constructed entirely from scrap. "That's a little work in progress," John Henry said mysteriously.

Finally, he wheeled her into a large shack. It was

ramshackle but clean and neat, with an eclectic collection of tables, lights, magnifiers, and tools. He opened a side door, revealing a bathroom large enough to accommodate a wheelchair.

"Very thoughtful," Sparks muttered.

John Henry continued as if he hadn't heard her sarcasm. "We fixed up another one for you at Uncle Joe's place, too. He's got a spare room all ready and—"

Sparks had had enough. She jerked her head around and looked up at him. "What exactly am I supposed to be doing here?" she asked, exasperated.

John Henry grinned enthusiastically. "Everything you did in the army. We're going to make our own counter-weapons to take out the ones on the street!"

"Are you crazy?" Sparks asked. "We don't have the army's resources."

"But we've got something they don't," John explained. "You!"

He pointed at her, but she stubbornly refused to complete their ritual. "You need a lot more than me."

Uncle Joe entered the workshop carrying a box. "You start making a list, darlin'," he said. "Folks call me Uncle Joe."

Joe looked at John Henry. "Don't just stand there, shorty, take the box." He winked slyly at the woman. "One thing about running a junkyard—people bring you the weirdest things."

John Henry opened the box. Sparks was astonished. "That's a mainframe IBM!"

Uncle Joe chuckled softly. "I-B-M, A-B-C . . . easy as one, two, three."

Sparks looked at him speculatively. "Where could you possibly have gotten . . . ?"

Uncle Joe was all big-eyed innocence. "Fella told me it fell off a truck, but it don't look too dented. If you knew how much stuff falls off trucks, you'd be in the junk game, too!"

A stunned Sparks nodded. "I'll . . . make a list."

A week later, John Henry stood in the junkyard, trying to enlarge Uncle Joe's makeshift forge. Uncle Joe walked up carrying Sparks's long list.

"She's something else," Uncle Joe said. "What's her story?"

As John Henry monkeyed with the forge, he explained that Sparks's mom was dead, and her dad drank himself in and out of rehab. "So she's on her own," he concluded.

Uncle Joe chuckled as he walked off. "Is she really?" he asked, barely loud enough for John to hear.

Inside her shack, Sparks organized the equipment. She had found that straightening her work area often helped organize her mind. And right now she had to think.

She had a rough idea how to miniaturize some components. Now all she needed was to work out the details. But the ideas just weren't coming.

She wiped her forehead. "Maybe it's the heat," she muttered to herself. "What this place really needs is an air conditioner."

Then she laughed. Maybe she'd mention it to Uncle Joe. She rolled her wheelchair over to the door for a breath of fresh air.

And there, in the middle of the junkyard, was John Henry, his shirt off, sweat glistening off his muscles as he worked at the newly enlarged forge. Sparks watched him from the doorway of her workshop.

He was slaving day and night, driving himself mercilessly to complete his new mission, one that he hoped would save lives. And he had shared this goal with her, she realized.

He had given her a purpose. He had saved her sanity, maybe even her life. She thought no one had ever had a better friend.

"Wimp," she muttered to herself. She turned away from the door and rolled back to her computers. If Johnny could work in this heat, then so could she.

Across town at Dantastic, Nathaniel Burke watched from a shadowed corner of the room as Lamont, the tough street kid, showed Martin the slick video arcade manufacturing facility. Martin's falling for everything he's shown, Burke observed, running a finger over his scarred cheek. Reeling him in was going to be almost too easy.

"This place is awesome!" Martin bubbled excitedly. "I'm going to own a spot like this one day."

"That's why I'm trying to get you a job here," Lamont said.

Martin grinned. "So what's up with this job, anyway?"

"The dude that runs this place is large," Lamont said. "I want you to meet him."

"Then call me Mr. Large!" said a voice behind them.

Martin and Lamont turned as Burke stepped out from behind a stack of boxes. "You must be Martin," Burke said. "I've heard a lot about you."

He turned to Lamont and shot him a sharp look. "I'll take over from here," he said.

"Sure thing, Mr. Large," Lamont said, giving him a conspiratorial smile and a thumbs-up.

As Lamont walked off, Burke put his arm around Martin. "I understand you want to work here."

The shack workroom was well equipped now. Sparks sat in her wheelchair, struggling to modify a large component rack.

Doing this from a wheelchair is a real pain, she thought. She reached for one tool and knocked another off the counter. She made a grab for it and, overbalanced by the component rack, she toppled out of her wheelchair.

"Blast!" she muttered. "Blast . . . BLAST . . . BLAST!" She slammed the floor angrily with her fist.

From out in the yard, John heard the noise and came running. He saw Sparks on the floor, struggling to collect the rack and fallen tool. He started to go help her, but something held him back.

Sparks's mouth was grim and determined as she snagged the fallen tool and shoved it onto the counter.

Then she pushed the rack up. Then, slowly, painfully, she pulled herself back onto her chair and breathed a sigh of satisfaction. She felt John Henry's eyes on her.

She wheeled her chair around slowly. Looking him in the eye, she grinned widely over her victory.

Gadgets

The forge was heated to maximum. John Henry stood before it, bare to the waist, pounding a thin plate of hot steel.

Wham! He hit the steel with a hammer. *Wham!*

"You work half the night here. Don't you ever get tired?" Sparks asked.

"Yeah . . . but then I think of who might get blasted by those weapons. What cop. What kid."

He put down his hammer and turned to her. "How're you doing, Sparky? You got everything you need?"

Sparks took a deep breath. "Yeah. Thanks for everything. And for *not* helping me with everything."

John Henry nodded. She pointed her finger at him. He reached his finger out. They had almost touched when a voice behind them shouted, "Johnny, Grandma wants you to bring everybody to check out her 'Cajun catfish stuffed with crawdaddy mousse and served à l'orange.' Whatever that is."

Sparks's eyes widened. "That . . . is an amazing concept," she said.

Martin stared around the workshop. "What're you guys making?"

John Henry wiped his hands on a paper towel. "Just gadgets."

Martin's eyes narrowed knowingly. "Top-secret stuff, huh?"

John Henry turned away to hide his grin. "Yeah, actually it is." He wadded up his paper towel, aimed carefully, lobbed it toward the trash can—and missed.

He shrugged. "You two go ahead, " he said. "I'll be up in a minute."

Sparks wheeled her chair out the door beside Martin. "How's your new job?" she asked.

Martin grinned excitedly. "It's dope! The boss made me his main man. Said if I studied up, I could make 'mad cream'!"

"If that's what you're in it for," Sparks said.

Martin's eyes glinted as he said, "C-R-E-A-M. That's Cash Rules Everything Around Me. Cream!"

Sparks laughed as she shook her head. "Some things money can't buy," she told him.

"What it can't get, I can't use," Martin said. Then he grinned widely. "You'd rule at my job, Sparks. John Henry says you're a genius with electronics."

Sparks smiled. "John Henry exaggerates," she said. But she didn't think she'd had a nicer compliment.

For all of them, the next months passed swiftly.

Sparks wore surgical magnifiers over her eyes and worked intently. On the basis of the principles she and John had discovered in the military, she made a series of modifications to some unusual weapons.

A tangle of small but useful electronic devices and a battery of mismatched equipment littered the counters.

She watched Uncle Joe strengthen the geodesic dome with steel plates, then weld on junk until it looked like a giant pile of metal. No one would ever guess there was a large, airy room beneath.

But it was John Henry she loved to watch: Measuring powdered chemicals. Mixing them with steel. Stirring his cauldrons. And sometimes smiling grimly as he pictured where all of this would lead.

But Sparks liked it best when he pounded at the anvil, with strange, blue-white sparks flying around him and the alloyed steel taking shape beneath his hammer!

Finally, after months of hard work, standing beneath the high arch of the geodesic dome, John Henry fitted a thin plate of curved steel around his arm. Then he fitted another piece against his upper leg. He looked up at Sparks and Uncle Joe and said, "Soon we'll be ready!"

Sparks's shack had grown into a state-of-the-art electronics lab. A little homey, a little piecemeal, but to her it was beautiful. John Henry and Uncle Joe waited expectantly to see what she had created.

She handed John a tiny piece of plastic. "Stick it in your ear," she said.

Filled with curiosity, he did as Sparks said. She put on a phone headset. "How do you read?" she asked.

John Henry grinned. "Five by five. Is this a receiver?"

"*Trans*ceiver," Sparks corrected him smugly. "Sends *and* receives. So watch what you say about me. It works within a radius of twenty miles. So does this."

She handed him a button-sized object with a small battery pack. She pointed at one of the monitors displaying a sharply detailed fish-eye image of John Henry's face as he looked into the tiny camera.

"Video, too!" John Henry was amazed. Sparks *had* been busy. Then he noticed a heavy stainless steel sledgehammer leaning against a counter.

As he lifted the heavy hammer it glistened almost magically. "What's this?" he asked.

"It was Joe's idea!" Sparks said. "After all, a man named John Henry has to have a hammer. But I designed it to do more than pound things."

John Henry looked at the excited faces of Sparks and Uncle Joe. "I have one last piece to make," he said.

John Henry watched the forge glow bright with molten metal and sighed. He had wanted to stay away from weapons work. But sometimes it was necessary to fight fire with fire.

From the forge he drew a fearsome mask of glowing steel—a helmet that would protect his head and conceal the top half of his face.

He examined it carefully, then plunged it into a tub of icy water. It hissed and squeaked. When he lifted it out it was gleaming, stainless and cold.

Sparks and Uncle Joe stood nearby, watching. Joe nodded. "So . . . John Henry *Irons* has turned himself into *steel.*"

John Henry said, "I think now's the time for a little test."

Steel

A well-dressed man and woman hurried along a downtown sidewalk. Behind them, Los Angeles glittered against the night sky. But there was danger in the shadows.

Suddenly, a wiry hand slammed them against the wall. "Give me all your cash," a voice growled. "I got a knife. Don't make me use it!"

The man handed over his wallet. The woman held out her purse. "Here. Just don't hurt us," she said.

The mugger snatched up his loot. He shoved the couple hard, then dashed off, leaving them sprawled on the pavement.

He ducked into an alley, ripped open the purse, and tossed aside a stack of photos and papers. What he wanted was the money.

"Not a nice way to treat somebody's family pictures," said a deep voice.

The mugger's head snapped up. Before him, blocking his exit, was a dark shape that glinted as shiny metal caught the light.

"Who are you, man? Get back or you're dead," the mugger threatened.

The dark shape said, "Just give them back their money, and we won't have a problem."

"I ain't got no problem!" The ratty mugger's voice quavered.

"Oh, yes, you do," the deep voice assured him.

An ambulance sped past the alley. Silhouetted against its flashing lights, the mugger saw the dark shape of an armored giant seven feet tall, maybe taller, wearing form-fitting armor of shining stainless steel!

The mugger froze in a state of near panic. "St-steel," he stammered. "You're all . . . steel!"

Over the small transceiver in his ear, John Henry heard Sparks giggle. "Surprise!" she hooted.

She's watching on the TV monitor, John Henry realized. She, too, could see the mugger's jaw almost hitting the pavement at the sight of him. If it hadn't been so serious, he might have smiled himself.

The mugger stared, cornered. Then he tried to run past.

He was collared by a metal-covered fist, lifted high off the ground, and slammed against the wall.

"Hang around a minute," the metal giant rumbled. He raised his other fist, aimed his wrist bracelet, and fired. A spike flew from the bracelet and rammed through the mugger's jacket, pinning him to the wall.

"Don't kill me! Don't kill me!" the mugger screamed in genuine terror.

"Remember how it feels," thundered the steel avenger. "Do it again . . . and you won't get off so lightly!"

The mugger's head bobbed as he frantically nodded his understanding. "Yes, sir, Steel-man! Anything you say!"

Again John Henry heard Sparks's exultant voice. "Congratulations, Johnny! I think he just got religion. And he figured out your name!"

"Can you believe this? Nine-one-one is busy!" The voice of the mugger's male victim rose with fury as he pounded on the pay phone. "How can I report this if—"

Then he noticed that his wife was staring up over his head. "What is it—?"

He turned and found himself gazing into the chest of a towering metal giant. The giant held out the purse and wallet. "I think these belong to you," his voice rumbled. "Tell the police the mugger is nailed to an alley wall by Sid's Deli. And on behalf of the citizens of L.A., I'd like to apologize. Y'all be cool!"

The man reached out gingerly and took the wallet and purse. "Uh . . . thank you . . . Mr.—"

"Steel!" said the giant. As the couple watched, he stepped back into the shadows and seemed to disappear.

From a nearby alley, Steel spoke to Sparks softly over the transceiver. "Did you see everything?"

"And taped it so you can watch the reruns." The excitement in Sparks's voice mirrored his own. "Oscilloscope monitors show your body temp's up a little. We've got to think about more ventilation."

"I'm fine," Steel said. And it was true. He'd never felt better.

Uncle Joe's voice cut in. "Police scanner's talking about a gang fight heating up off Hill Street."

Sparks cut in quickly. "Whoa, guys. Let's not bite off more than we can chew the first time out."

Steel grinned. "Hey, Uncle Joe, give me a cross street!"

John Henry Irons (Shaquille O'Neal) is a lieutenant in the United States Army. He is a member of a special team developing a weapon that will save lives by stunning the enemy, not killing them.

Nathaniel Burke (Judd Nelson) was on John Henry's army team — until Nathaniel was dishonorably discharged.

Susan Sparks (Annabeth Gish) is John Henry's best friend. She was also a member of the team, until Nathaniel's twisted ambition crippled her for life.

Uncle Joe (Richard Roundtree) is an important person in John Henry Irons' life.

John Henry and Nathaniel prepare to demonstrate the new weapon to an important senator.

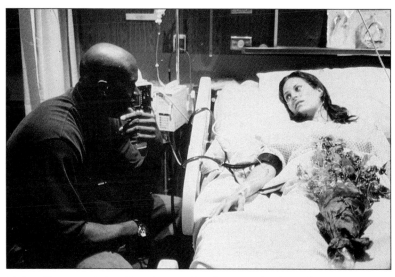

John Henry visits Sparks in the hospital after the weapon demonstration goes terribly wrong.

John Henry becomes STEEL.

Grandma Odessa (Irma P. Hall) always encourages John Henry to do what is right.

STEEL and Sparks join forces to fight evil.

John Henry wants nothing more than to be a good role model to his brother Martin (Ray Jay Norwood).

Watch Your Back!

Three teenagers, wearing the black gang colors that marked them as Skins, sprinted through Pershing Square Park. Behind them, a low-rider car careened around a corner. "I see them!" a voice from the car shouted.

The car came straight at the Skins. Another teenager, wearing the green gang colors of the Reefs, leaned out the car window, aiming a pistol. There was no way the Skins could outrun bullets. They knew they were dead.

Suddenly they heard the Reefs' car screech to a halt. They glanced over their shoulders, wondering what had saved them.

Lit by the car's headlights, a metal giant stood in the center of the road, blocking the vehicle's path.

The Reef gunman hung out the window, waving his pistol, shouting, "Move out the way, fool! This is our 'hood!"

Steel scowled. "Put the gun down and there won't be any trouble."

The gunman rolled his eyes. "Man, please. I'm the one with the firepower!" To prove it, he leveled the pistol at Steel's chest and pulled the trigger.

Steel stood there, unaffected, as a half-dozen bullets hit, splattered, sparked, and ricocheted off his armor.

Through the transceiver, he heard Uncle Joe mutter, "Do I wanna look?"

Sparks quavered, "One of us has to!"

"I'm fine," Steel murmured softly. "I made the armor, remember. I know what it can do."

"Tell that to my heart," Sparks said.

The Reef driver slammed the car into gear. "Ram him," he said.

Steel reached over his shoulder and drew his hammer from its sheath.

From inside the car, the Reef driver scoffed. "What's the Steel Man gonna do? Hit us with his little hammer?"

Steel slung the hammer head against his shoulder as if it were a rifle. His steel-gloved thumb found the selector slide switch on the hammer's shaft.

"Sonic is forward, right?" he muttered.

Sparks yelled into the transceiver. "Yeah, yeah, forward! Forward!"

Steel grinned. "Then it's hammer time!" The trigger mechanism popped down into place. His finger closed on it. He aimed and fired!

Ka-vwooooom!

A shock wave of sound hit the dusty low-rider, slamming it to a stop. The back end buckled up like it had hit a wall! The sudden movement sent the Reef driver and gunman crashing forward through the windshield and onto the street.

The dazed Reefs looked up, bleary-eyed, at the monolithic Steel.

"You guys should always buckle up," he chastised them.

Four other heavily armed Reefs bailed out of the back. Two dashed to one side, the other two cocked automatic weapons and pointed them at Steel's chest.

Steel knew that if he didn't do something fast, he would be caught in a hail of bullets. And while they couldn't penetrate his armor, the teens might get hurt by the ricochets. He grasped the shaft of his hammer and tripped a tiny red switch. The built-in electromagnet in the head of the hammer engaged.

The hammer head smacked tightly against Steel's armor, magnetizing it. A barrage of rifles, handguns, knives, even a pair of metal-frame eyeglasses, flew toward him and slammed against his armor with a series of satisfying *klangs*!

Watching her monitor, Sparks couldn't stop laughing. "What a magnetic personality!" she chortled into the transceiver as four of the Reefs turned tail and ran.

Beside her, a police scanner crackled out the order, "Pershing Square. Shots fired. Code three."

Sparks spoke into the transceiver. "Johnny, you're about to have official company. Cops are coming!"

Steel clicked off the magnet and the objects stuck to him fell in a pile at his feet. In his ear, he heard Sparks shout a warning, "Watch your back!"

Steel pivoted and swung his hammer, sweeping two diehard Reefs off their feet, breaking the bats they wielded. They lay there, not daring to move. One of them muttered, "He's got eyes in the back of his head!"

Steel looked down at the teenagers. "And I'll be watching you. So clean up your act. Now make like a rash and break out."

Steel didn't have to tell them twice. They ran, glad to get away alive.

"Good looking out, Sparky!" Steel said.

"Hey, be my legman, I'll only have eyes for you," she quipped.

"Funny lady—!" Steel was about to say more when a squad car screamed into the park. Two others screeched in behind him.

Uncle Joe watched the monitors. "Does he know a way out of this?" he asked anxiously.

Sparks tried to be reassuring. "Oh, yeah. I'm sure he does. I hope."

Through the windows of their squad cars, the cops exchanged confused glances. They had never seen anything like this man in armor before. No one had.

They climbed out and leveled their pistols at him.

Sergeant Johnson, the senior cop, a serious career officer, spoke over a loudspeaker.

"Okay, Sir Lancelot, step away from those weapons. And get those hands up! *Way* up!"

Steel obediently stepped away from the weapons . . .

and toward one of the buildings that ringed the park. As he raised his hands, his wrist bracelets ratcheted around to a new chamber.

Aiming the chamber upward, he fired. A spike shot out, trailing a thin wire. It shot up three stories and embedded itself in the roof.

Steel keyed a switch and his wristband whirled, retracting the wire and whipping him up off the ground.

The cops watched in amazement as he flew up toward the roof. Young Officer Woods whistled admiringly. "Man, you didn't have to put them up *that* high," he said.

Sergeant Johnson was disgusted. "What are you guys standing around for? After him!" he yelled.

On the rooftop, Steel looked around, then sprinted to the far edge. He stopped, gauging the distance between buildings.

In his ear, Sparks yelled, "The range finder says it's too far! Don't even think about jumping, Johnny!"

Steel grinned. "Piece o' cake, Sparky. In high school I finished second in the long jump," he said as he moved back from the roof's edge. Then he started to run.

Sparks shouted in his ear, "Don't put your macho attitude up against my computer! You weren't wearing seventy-five pounds of armor then!"

But Steel wasn't listening. He was sailing out across the gap toward the building beyond.

Only he didn't make it. He barely managed to grab the roof's edge with his hands. He hung, panting, over the abyss.

"Okay, Sparks. One for the computer," Steel said. Muscles straining, he hauled himself onto the roof.

The cops appeared on the building behind him. Johnson shouted, "There he is!"

"No time to breathe . . . keep going!" Sparks yelled.

Steel fired another cable, then jumped off the roof. He fell in a controlled descent, trailing a wire from his wrist band as he was lowered swiftly toward the ground.

"Thirty feet to go," Sparks said. "Twenty . . ."

Then the wire snapped! Steel plummeted toward the concrete below.

Work in Progress

Steel landed amid a collection of trash cans. Hard.

"Johnny? Johnny, are you all right?" Sparks's voice screamed in his ear.

Steel sat up, shaking his head to clear it. "A little trashed, that's all," he mumbled.

Sparks sighed with relief. "Guess I better do some more work on the wire's tensile strength."

"That would be nice," Steel murmured as he staggered to his feet.

"Hey, it's a work in progress," Sparks said in his ear.

He picked up a piece of armor that had fallen off his thigh and limped behind a Dumpster just as a squad car swerved into the far end of the alley, siren wailing.

From the front seat, Johnson and Woods scanned the area. Overturned garbage cans and a big stack of cardboard boxes cluttered the alley. But no armored giant.

Suddenly the boxes exploded outward.

"Would you look at that!" Woods cried.

Steel blazed from the tangle of boxes and past their squad car. He was riding a fluid, thoroughly redesigned motorcycle, aerodynamically fitted with his special armor.

"After him, blast it!" Johnson roared.

Woods backed the squad car from the alley and screamed after the armored giant.

As Steel streaked through city streets like a silver comet, the squad car followed in hot pursuit.

"Y'gotta admit, the guy's got style," Woods said.

Johnson glanced at him sharply. "Just get the plate number," he growled.

Woods struggled to read the bike's license through binoculars as the squad car bounced. "Looks like . . . Sierra, Tango, Echo, Echo, Lima," he read. "STEEL. Well, duh."

Steel was pulling away from the squad car when the traffic light ahead went from green to yellow. He barely made it through. But in the intersection up ahead, the signal turned red and there was cross-traffic.

Steel yelled, "Sparky? The lights! Do something!"

"I see it," she replied. "Hold on. I'm typing as fast as I can!"

Her computer screen flashed detailed grid maps of the L.A. traffic system. The adjacent monitor showed Steel's

live point of view as he closed in on the crowded
intersection. Suddenly her control panel went dark.

"Uh-oh," Sparks said.

"'Uh-oh'?! I don't want to hear 'uh-oh'!" Steel yelled.

Uncle Joe smacked the side of the computer rack.
Everything lit back up. Sparks glanced at him gratefully.

"Just kidding, Johnny. We're cool," she said.

Steel had slowed his bike, but he was almost at the
cross streets and the squad car was getting closer. And
now the traffic signal was flashing *all* of its lights. "No,
we're not!" he shouted.

"Hey, it ain't easy being green," Sparks said. She
tapped a final key. "There!"

Steel's light turned a solid green. Cross-traffic drivers hit
their brakes and Steel shot through the intersection like a
bolt of lighting.

"Now this should close the door," Sparks muttered. She
tapped a key and the signal went red. The cross-traffic
resumed.

The pursuing squad car swerved madly, clipping the
rear bumper of a civilian car.

Sergeant Johnson seethed, choosing to ignore the
quirky grin that split Officer Woods's face.

As Steel whipped around the corner and made his final
run for home, Sparks spoke into the transceiver. "I should
be able to give you green all the way!"

Several blocks ahead of Steel, Grandma Odessa and
Martin were waiting at the crosswalk. The red light turned
to green and the green light turned red without even

going to yellow first. Cars screeched to a stop and a roar filled the street. They watched, dazzled, as Steel streaked past!

The bike's engine was sputtering as Steel cut sharply into an alley. Ahead of him was a tall wooden fence.

Sparks hit a switch and a hidden gate snapped open. Steel flashed through and it snapped shut behind him.

Coming from behind, Johnson's squad car sped into the empty alley and slammed on its brakes. Sergeant Johnson was furious. "Air Ten, where the blazes are you?" he shouted into his mike.

A police helicopter thundered over the top of a nearby building. The voice of its pilot crackled over Johnson's radio. "Right behind you. We'll spot him," the pilot said.

From the streets below, Steel heard the chopper as he headed straight for the huge mound of scrap metal piled in the center of the junkyard.

Sparks keyed a switch and a section of the scrap heap yawned open like a small garage door. It was a false front that Uncle Joe had sculpted. Once closed, it would be undetectable.

Steel and his bike disappeared inside.

The police chopper swept its searchlight over the quiet junkyard. "Nobody in here," the pilot said. "I'm swinging north."

In their squad car, Johnson and Woods looked at each other, stymied.

"Where'd he go?" Johnson grumbled.

Woods looked at him. With a perfectly straight face he answered, "The Batcave?"

Who Is Steel?

The interior of the dome erupted with joy. Steel, Sparks, and Uncle Joe laughed and exchanged high fives. They all talked at once.

"Man, I haven't felt this good since the Dodgers won the series in '65," Uncle Joe chortled.

"Did you see the faces on those kids?" John Henry asked.

"They acted like they got religion, that's for sure," Joe said.

John Henry laughed. "Man, when that wire pulled me up, my heart dropped!"

"And when it broke, my heart *stopped*!" Sparks said.

"Work in progress," John Henry and Sparks said together, laughing uproariously.

Sparks and Joe helped John Henry take off his armor. His muscular body was bruised and soaked with sweat.

"Uh, excuse me," Sparks said, "but next time, please trust my range finder before you jump, okay?"

Joe chuckled. "Good thing this armor's stainless, otherwise you'd be rusting."

"The bike needs tuning," John Henry said. He stood as he toweled off, too juiced to sit still for long.

"Quite a few things need tuning," Sparks said. "I've got a printout coming so we can evaluate everything."

John Henry looked her in the eyes. "Sparky, I don't know what I'd do without you. You're all that!" He pointed at her.

She lightly touched his fingertip. "Really?" she asked softly.

He wanted her to know how much she meant to him. "No doubt," he said.

John Henry tore his eyes away from hers. "C'mon, Uncle Joe, let's take a look at the bike," he said.

He rolled up the towel he'd been using, aimed carefully, lobbed it toward the laundry basket—and missed. Naturally.

Martin couldn't wait to get to Dantastic to tell the other interns and techies what he'd seen. "This armored giant came jetting past us, doing like eighty!" he said. "The cop car—"

Burke placed an arm on his shoulder. "Morning, Martin. I hear you're interested in the new microchip game technology," he said.

Martin turned to him with a big grin. "Yeah. I think that new interactive unit sounds—"

"Fly?" Burke suggested. "Let's you and me have a look." Keeping an arm around the boy's shoulder, Burke asked confidentially, "You really saw that man in—"

"Steel!" Martin's eyes glowed with excitement. "Yeah. Last night. He was tight. Got some skills. And he's a brother."

"Really?" Burke asked. "Think he was from your neighborhood?"

Martin laughed. "Well, he sure isn't from Beverly Hills!"

Mr. Large had a lot of questions. About Martin's neighborhood. About where he lived. About his family.

And Martin answered them all proudly. He didn't notice when Daniels's sinister eyes met Burke's over his head.

It seemed to Grandma Odessa that all anyone in the neighborhood could talk about was Steel. What his armor looked like. What kind of motorcycle he rode. What he might want. Who he might be.

Even the grocer had his small portable TV tuned to a news program about the armored giant. The couple who had been mugged explained how Steel had recovered their belongings. "He was seven-foot-six. Big as a mountain!" the man described.

Grandma Odessa left the grocery store looking very thoughtful.

Burke and the eye-patched gang leader, Slats, met in sun-drenched Echo Park. They sat on a bench near a hot dog vendor, watching the lake reflect the city skyline.

Slats fingered a brand-new heavy gold chain.

"Nice chain. Big," Burke said.

"We're getting paid. What's wrong with a little flossing, man?" he asked.

Burke sneered. "Floss too much, and the wrong people will notice. Maybe I better let somebody else ride in my Bankmobile. Maybe you'll end up like Cutter."

Burke stared pointedly at Slats, who grudgingly pocketed the chain.

Burke handed the teenager a thick manila envelope. "Singer will pick you and your men up. Stay precisely on schedule," he said.

Slats smiled. "How much we withdrawing?"

Burke smiled crookedly. "More than you can imagine. Now, what's the buzz on this Steel guy?"

Slats snorted. "Sounds like a tin man on steroids to me!"

Burke stood up to leave. "Never underestimate your enemy," he said. "And keep the gold out of sight."

The Steel Mobile was on patrol. At least that's what Joe called it. Joe sat behind the wheel of his dusty junk van, with his golden retriever, Lillie, riding shotgun. Steel rode in back.

Sparks's voice, yawning, came over their radio. "Five nights and still no sign of those weapons."

Back at the dome, Sparks attached a canister to her wheelchair. Her police scanner crackled with calls. Various oscilloscopes flickered as they tracked John Henry's respiration and heart rate. Monitors showed the van's position on the L.A. street grid and a point of view from behind Uncle Joe and Lillie in the truck.

Sparks yawned again. "I like having the time to make improvements on my chair but—hey, what do you guys think about some wallpaper in here?"

Steel leaned up beside Joe. "Hey, Sparky. Stay on point, you hear? I feel it. Something's going to pop."

—▪——

Not far away, the dark Humvee rounded a corner, right on schedule. Singer hopped out, wearing a black jump-suit and carrying a satchel. He ran toward a manhole, jacked it open, and dropped inside.

In a utilities service tunnel below street level, he opened the satchel, removed a large explosive device, and set it on the floor. Then he quickly climbed out of the manhole, replaced the cover, and hopped into the Humvee. The armored vehicle inched forward, rolling one wheel squarely atop the manhole.

Beneath the Humvee's wheel, the bomb went off concussively. Smoke streaked out of the small openings in the manhole cover, but the Humvee's heavy wheel held it in place.

The street lights went dark.

—▪——

Inside the dome, one of Sparks's monitors began flashing a quadrant of L.A. Another monitor showed an infrared satellite image of L.A. from space. She tweaked the image larger.

Sparks spoke tensely into her mike. "Heads up. Something's cooking. The city's emergency services interlink shows a major telephone and power failure near Hope and Wilshire. I'm zeroing in on it through the LandSat satellite to see if our eye in the sky spots anything."

Steel's voice answered, "We'll check it out."

In his secret, high-tech command center in Dantastic's subbasement, Burke sat behind his desk with his ear pressed to a phone, rubbing his scar. A tough-looking mercenary named Jake, wearing headphones, studied the monitors and switches that lined the wall.

From nearby, Daniels spoke through the toothpick in his mouth, "Time for our infomercial?"

Burke looked at his watch and nodded to Jake, who threw several switches. "First thing is to cut out the cops," he said.

Inside the dome, a burst of static wiped out the transmissions from Sparks's police scanners. Sparks twisted some dials, but all she got was more static.

Sparks shouted into her transceiver, "Johnny? Do you read? Hello?"

Inside the junk van, all that came over the radio was static. Then Sparks's voice came through loud and clear. ". . . switching to FM-shielded sideband. Do you read now?"

"I read you, five by five. What happened?" Steel asked.

"Jamming. Police frequencies are out, too. Big disturbance at Sixth and Hope! Something's going down—oh, no!" Sparks answered tensely.

Steel felt a rush of excitement. "What's up?"

"Whoever they are, they're hitting L.A.'s biggest ATM," Sparks answered. "The Federal Reserve Bank!"

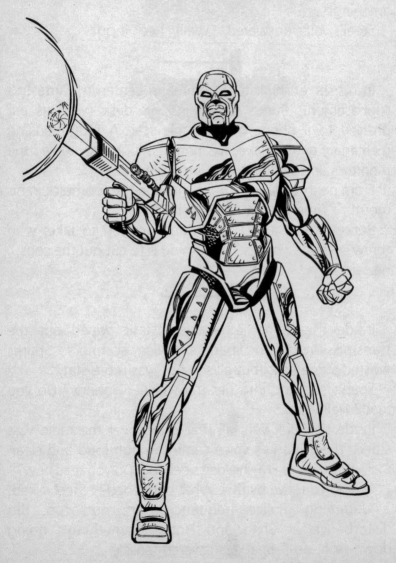

Time's Up

The Federal Reserve Bank sat on the corner—a monolithic, formidable building, well protected by its solid concrete walls.

The Humvee slowly rounded a corner. "Target in sight," Singer said, squinting through the darkened windshield. Slats pulled on his hood. A small TV camera popped up from the roof of the Humvee and panned around slowly.

In Burke's secret command center, a video monitor showed the Humvee's view of the bank.

"Phones and alarms are down," Jake said.

Burke snapped the order, "Proceed!"

A small port opened in the Humvee's armored side. The muzzle of the sonic cannon appeared.

Ka-va-boom! A battering ram of low sound shattered the concrete side of the building, and a section of the wall collapsed.

The thieves could see the steel vault inside.

A laser seared out from the cannon, splattering molten drops as it carved through the vault.

Slats, Holdecker, and several other masked Marks jumped from the Humvee just as two bank guards came rushing around a corner. Slats fired a burst of energy from his rifle. The guards flew back and lay still.

The thieves jumped across the rubble and through the fissure opened by the laser in the side of the vault. Their hot Xenotech flashlights knifed through the smoke and dust, illuminating dozens of large pallets, stacked five feet high with bundles of newly printed hundred-dollar bills.

Holdecker whistled. "There must be a zillion dollars in here!"

"You know the drill," Slats snapped. "Suck up all you can in ninety seconds."

Hurriedly the thieves scooped the bills into duffel bags.

Right on schedule, Slats shouted, "Time's up! Let's get out of here!" But as the gang raced for the rubble-strewn exit, a burst of roiling energy suddenly exploded before them! A gleaming colossus stepped forward, blocking their path.

Slats gulped. "It's Steel! Ice his metal butt!" he shouted.

Two thieves leveled their pulse rifles and fired.

Steel was struck full in the chest, and Slats raised his fist in a sign of victory.

Then his jaw dropped. The energy bounced off of Steel's armor onto a nearby pickup truck, engulfing it in flames!

"What about using the magnet on those guns?" Sparks asked in Steel's ear.

"The alloy in those weapons is nonmagnetic," Steel answered.

There was an embarrassed pause. Then Sparks said, "I knew that."

From his command center, Burke watched Steel on the monitors. "Who's he talking to?" Burke asked.

Jake twisted some monitor controls. "I'm scanning for it, sir," he said.

Steel leveled his hammer and fired a laser at a half-broken, hanging concrete sign. It dropped, knocking the guns out of the hands of two of the thieves.

Steel fired at the Humvee's tires, but the static bursts bounced off its armor.

"The Humvee's got armor like yours, Johnny!" Sparks said in his ear.

Steel aimed the shaft of his hammer at the thieves and flicked the selector switch. Exploding pellets landed in front of Slats and his gang, clouding the area. The gang started to cough. "Tear gas!" Holdecker yelled.

Slats shouted, "Jump in the van! Go!" He scrambled in and the others dove after him.

Steel dodged roiling energy fired by the recovering gang members. One static burst bounced off him. He heard Sparks's voice through the transceiver. "You're about to get the blues, Johnny!"

Steel heard the wail of police sirens.

From the back of the Humvee, Slats growled, "Who is that fool?"

Singer calmly hit a switch. "A dead man," he said.

The Humvee's rear window snapped down and the sonic muzzle of the cannon thrust out of it.

Va-woom! The sonic shock wave hit Steel, blowing him backward into the air. He rammed into a sidewalk news kiosk, shattering it.

"Johnny! Are you all right?" Sparks yelled in his ear.

Steel's ribs felt broken. His chin was bloody.

"I'm fine," he said.

Police cars screeched to a stop, blocking the road and surrounding him.

Officers Johnson and Woods jumped out, squinting through the smoke and tear gas, trying to see what was happening. A police chopper roared overhead.

"You're out-gunned, Johnny! Bail!" Sparks said in his ear.

In his command monitor, Burke saw the helicopter hovering over the robbery site. It was just what he needed for his final demonstration. "Hit it!" he said into the phone.

A roof panel on the Humvee whipped open. Slats aimed his pulse rifle upward and fired.

An instant later, the chopper's cockpit exploded and the helicopter spun out of control.

Struggling to his feet, Steel saw the helicopter plummeting toward Sergeant Johnson. He leaped, tackling Johnson to safety just as the flaming wreckage crashed onto the spot where the officer had been standing.

Johnson looked at Steel's bleeding chin, then through the gleaming mask into the dark eyes of the man who had just saved his life.

The Humvee peeled out, opening fire, plowing through squad cars. Cops dove for cover.

Steel nodded grimly at Johnson. Then, fighting the pain in his side, he rose to his feet and sped off around the corner. He vaulted onto the seat of his idling motorcycle, gunned it, and roared away.

Behind him, a squad car rounded the corner in hot pursuit.

Sparks spoke into Steel's ear. "Turn right up ahead!"

Steel gunned the bike around a corner and saw the squad car swing in behind him. His metal-gloved finger found a button on the bike's hand grip and pressed it. The bike's tailgate opened, spraying a broad fan of tacks out onto the street behind him. The squad car hit them and all four tires blew out.

Steel was breathing hard now and could feel himself weakening. He knew his condition would show clearly on Sparks's oscilloscopes.

"Hang in there, Johnny," Sparks said reassuringly in his ear. "Take the next left. You'll see the rabbit hole."

Steel almost ran his shoulder along the ground making the turn. Then he saw Uncle Joe's old van moving slowly just ahead, its back ramp down and dragging.

Steel drove his motorcycle up the ramp and into the van. The ramp slammed shut behind him.

From a view hole in the back, Steel saw a squad car come screaming at the van. Then it roared on past.

They were safe, at least for now.

The Infomercial

Inside Burke's command center, Jake turned away from his monitor. "Steel stopped transmitting before I could triangulate, but I got some parameters," he said.

"Good," Burke said. "Find Steel's home base." He handed Jake a stack of videotapes. "And send these to the TV stations right away."

Inside a cinderblock room decorated with a large flag bearing a Nazi swastika, a group of skinheads gathered around a TV, watching the sonic cannon destroy the outer wall of the Federal Reserve Bank.

Their leader, lounging beside a rack of guns, grinned appreciatively. "I want those weapons!" he demanded.

In Africa, a French mercenary, cleaning his rifle, watched a small, battery-powered TV. He whistled appreciatively as the news from L.A. showed a laser slicing cleanly through a metal bank vault.

The mercenary called for his lieutenant. "Find out who makes these new toys."

In Colombia, a drug lord propped his feet on the side of his yacht as his television flashed images of the shattered helicopter hurtling toward the ground.

He spoke into a cellular phone. "Find out how we can get those weapons. Pronto!"

Among America's criminal underworld, the weapons were discussed almost endlessly. "Whoever created those guns isn't going to be selling them on street corners," an overlord's assistant declared.

"Where, then?" the overlord snapped.

The assistant smiled knowingly.

Flesh and Blood

Under the dome, Sparks and Uncle Joe helped John Henry remove his armor.

Sparks flinched as she lifted away his chest plate. The skin over his ribs was pulped and bloody. "You may be steel on the outside, but you're still flesh and blood underneath," she said.

"*Too* much blood, looks like," Uncle Joe announced.

John Henry grimaced as Sparks dabbed iodine on his cuts. "I'm okay. It's just a scratch."

"Cut the macho garbage," Sparks growled at him. "Your ribs are broken!"

John Henry noticed he was having trouble breathing. He sighed. "You're right, Sparky. I don't know if I can do this," he admitted.

Uncle Joe piled the armor to one side for cleaning. "It's

hard going, no question," he said. He dabbed carefully at John Henry's chin. "Just like what the ol' John Henry went through."

Sparks looked at Uncle Joe, her eyes flashing. "Yeah, and we know what happened to him."

Uncle Joe shook his head sadly. "That was back in 1871. John Henry was a steel driver, working to build something important, too—the Big Bend Tunnel on the Chesapeake & Ohio Railroad in West Virginia.

"In those days, steel drivers used long-handled hammers to pound steel drills into rock to make holes for blasting explosives. When an experimental steam drill was brought into the tunnel, John Henry knew it threatened the livelihood of the workers there. So he wagered that, using hammers, he could beat the steam drill in a race.

"Taking a twenty-pound hammer in each hand, he drilled two seven-foot holes in the time it took the steam drill to bore only one nine-foot hole. But then—a blood vessel burst in his brain.

"He died pounding steel, but he beat that ol' steam drill."

"But he died doing it!" Sparks insisted.

Uncle Joe smiled at Sparks. "Can't argue with you there. 'Course, he didn't have you to help him."

Sparks blinked. "That's got nothing to—" she started to argue.

John Henry interrupted. "Can I get some water?"

Uncle Joe handed him a paper cup.

"They've got a warrant out for you," Sparks told John Henry. "For 'the man in steel.' Some of the cops think you're part of that gang since you all had the same weapons. And somehow the TV stations got videotapes of the robbery."

John Henry gulped his water.

"I have a feeling Burke is behind this somehow," he said. "Who else could have gotten those weapons on the streets so fast, with modifications we'd discussed but never implemented?" He crumpled his cup angrily, lobbed it at a trash can—and missed. "I've got to find those weapons!" he said.

Sparks put her hands on her hips and said determinedly, "What you've got to do is get some sleep!"

At the Fifth Precinct, a sergeant manning the night desk answered the ringing phone. "Sergeant Croft, here."

"Good evening, Sergeant," a pleasant voice answered. "Would you like to know where to find the fancy weapon that brought down your helicopter?"

Sparks watched John Henry leave the dome, heading for home. She turned on Uncle Joe, demanding angrily, "Why are you pressing him so hard?"

Uncle Joe shrugged. "At the mill I always noticed how the iron that went through the hottest fire made the best quality steel at the other end."

Sparks frowned. "*If* it comes out the other end."

John Henry stuck his head into Grandma Odessa's kitchen. "Evening," he whispered. By now she had him and Martin well trained.

"Evening," Odessa whispered, looking up from her cookbook.

"Souffle?" John Henry asked.

Odessa nodded. "Gonna get it right if it kills me. What'd you do to your chin?"

John Henry felt his chin. "Must've bumped into something."

Grandma Odessa raised her eyebrows. "Did you? See any of that big robbery stuff on the TV?"

John Henry answered honestly. "On TV? No, ma'am."

Odessa bent over her cookbook and jotted a note. "Times are hard on the streets," she said. "Everybody feels like this big cloud's hanging over them. The only hope seems to be that Steel fellow. He's sure a big drink o' water. Tall. Like you."

John Henry started to back softly out of the kitchen. "Is he? Well, I think I'm going to get some sleep," he said.

As he turned, the kitchen light glinted off something shiny in his ear. "What's that in your ear, son?" Grandma Odessa asked.

John Henry felt the transceiver he had forgotten to remove. "In my ear?" he asked, stalling as he thought of an excuse. "Oh. I forgot about it. It's a little . . . um . . . hearing aid thing."

Odessa looked at him skeptically. "You never had a hearing problem," she said. "Now don't you play with me. I want the truth. Are you—?"

Her question was interrupted by a loud *crr-rash!* as a black-uniformed man wearing a black-visored helmet and clutching a rifle smashed through the kitchen window.

Odessa grabbed her rolling pin and hit him hard.

He dropped like a stone.

The back door flew open. Two more men in black uniforms charged into the kitchen.

John Henry slung one across the room and against the oven.

The oven door flew off, and a flattened souffle fell out.

Now Odessa was really mad. There was one uniformed man left standing. She tossed John Henry her big iron skillet, shouting, "Here! Smash him with this!"

The man crouched, pointing his rifle at John Henry's heart. "Police! Freeze!" he shouted.

Belatedly, John Henry realized that these weren't robbers, but members of an L.A. police SWAT team. He dropped the frying pan carefully.

"On the ground! Now!" the cop shouted.

Martin stumbled into the kitchen, rubbing sleep from his eyes. "Grandma? What's happening?"

The policeman pointed his gun at John Henry, shouting, "Do it!"

"I'm down, I'm down. Be cool," John Henry said. Cops swept in the door and pinned John Henry to the floor.

"This is a search warrant," a second policeman said, as he waved a paper. Police swept in, fanning out to search the apartment.

One of the cops handcuffed John Henry. "John Henry Irons, you're under arrest for suspicion of armed robbery, assault, and possession of illegal weapons," he said.

Odessa frowned ominously. "Johnny, what are they talking about?"

A cop entered the kitchen carrying a heat pulse rifle. "This was in the basement," he said.

John Henry was as stunned as Odessa and Martin. Martin traded a frightened glance with his grandmother as the officer continued reading John Henry his rights.

Get Me Out of Here!

John Henry stood against a wall in a lineup of six males, all of similar size and build.

The detective in charge called out, "Number One, step forward."

The first man in the lineup scowled but did as he was told.

From the darkened viewing room, the couple who were mugged looked at him carefully, then shook their heads. "Not tall enough," the man said.

The detective nodded. "Number Two, front and center."

Number Two stepped forward chuckling. "You got it! Man, I always wanted to be in *A Chorus Line*."

The detective wasn't impressed. "Put a lid on it, Number Two," he growled.

The woman looked at the detective anxiously. "You know, Steel was very kind to us. I'd hate to—"

The long-suffering detective sighed. "I know, ma'am. But you two saw him up close. And he has been implicated in some serious crimes."

"Two's not big enough. Detective, the man who helped us was masked. But he was on the right side of the law." The man glanced at his wife. His decision made, he added, "And he's not up there."

The detective was clearly annoyed. "All right, all right. Thanks for coming." He looked around. "Marcus? C'mere."

Sergeant Marcus Johnson stepped forward.

"You saw him real good, Marcus. Get in there and find him."

Sergeant Johnson walked into the lineup room. He started on the right, looking carefully at Number Six. He shook his head, then he scrutinized Number Five. "Nope," he said.

He stepped in front of John Henry. He saw the cut where Steel's chin had bled and looked into the eyes of the man who had saved his life.

Sergeant Johnson shook his head no and moved on to study the next man in the lineup.

With a *clang!* John Henry's jail cell slammed shut and he was left alone.

John Henry immediately started talking. "Okay. I'm back in my cell."

Sparks's voice whispered in his ear through the transceiver he still wore. "Why won't they let you come home?"

"They're holding me for questioning. National Security Administration's flying Colonel David in."

Sparks's voice brightened. "Maybe he'll be able to help."

An overworked guard peered in to see who the prisoner was talking to. Looked like he was talking to himself. The guard shrugged. You get all kinds of fruit-cakes here, he thought.

"Don't count on help from Colonel David. Did you check out what I said?"

"Yeah, the TV stations said the tapes of the robbery were sent anonymously," Sparks answered. Then she added sarcastically, "Big time infomercial—'High-tech weapons, not available in any store! And if you act now—'"

John Henry interrupted her. "How does a buyer make contact?"

Sparks snorted. "In this day and age? Only one way."

"The Internet," John Henry said. "You found it?"

"Of course!" Sparks sounded insulted that he would even ask. "Now the bad news: the big auction is going down in eleven hours."

"They give a location?" John Henry asked.

"Not until the last minute," Sparks said. "We need help from higher up, anyway. But that may take a while."

"I need to get out of here, Sparky," John said grimly.

John Henry could almost see Sparks's gleeful grin as she said confidently, "We're working on it!"

In his outer office, District Attorney Mitchell Litt signed his name on an electronic clipboard held out by a delivery man, then took the envelope he was handed.

The delivery man thanked him politely and walked out the door.

Uncle Joe grinned as he left the building. In the envelope, the DA would find a document from Publishers Clearing House telling him that he "might already be a winner." But what Uncle Joe had gotten back was worth more to him than millions.

He climbed into his van and attached the electronic clipboard to a cell phone. "Are you getting his signature?" he asked into the radio.

Sparks's voice answered. "Clear as a bell!"

The voice of Litt's secretary came over the intercom, interrupting his dream of millions. "Excuse me, sir. The mayor's office on one."

The DA sat a little straighter and picked up his phone. "Yes?" he said.

Sparks spoke into the phone while adjusting her computer. The screen flashed the message SAMPLING VOICE, and began recording the conversation.

"May I confirm who's speaking?" Sparks asked carefully.

"This is District Attorney Mitchell Litt," the DA said. Sparks smiled.

"I'm Connie Lavine with the mayor's office," Sparks lied. "He wanted to know if you are free this afternoon."

The DA's voice hesitated as he checked his schedule. Then he said, "It's pretty short notice, but I could be free by one o'clock."

The computer had what it needed. "Well, don't do anything yet, Mr. Litt," Sparks said. "I'll call back to confirm in a few minutes."

At the Fifth Precinct, the desk officer answered the ringing phone. "Hollenbeck Division. Davis."

"This is District Attorney Mitchell Litt," said a voice Officer Davis recognized.

"What can we do for you, sir?" Officer Davis asked.

At the dome, Sparks had propped a telephone next to her computer's speakers. She sat nearby, talking softly into a microphone.

"You're holding a prisoner there, John Henry Irons," she said. "It's pretty short notice, but I want him free by one o'clock."

Her computer flashed the message, VOICE BEING TRANSLATED.

A voice coming from the computer echoed her words, "You're holding a prisoner there, John Henry Irons. It's pretty short notice, but I want him free by one o'clock." It sounded exactly as if DA Litt had spoken the words.

On the other end of the line, Officer Davis said, "Of course, sir, but I'll need—"

The DA's voice cut him off impatiently. "Written authorization. It's coming over your fax now. My signature's on it."

At one o'clock, John Henry's cell door clanged open. He was free to go.

Sparks had done her job. Now it was time for him to do his.

Game's Up

Uncle Joe's deceptively grungy Steel Mobile chugged through midtown Los Angeles. As usual, the golden retriever, Lillie, rode shotgun. Steel, fully armored, sat grimly in the back. Sparks followed their progress on her monitors.

"Have you connected with the colonel?" Steel asked her tensely.

"Anonymously, through a satellite link so they can't trace it here," Sparks told him. Colonel David and his men would be waiting at the police helipad until Steel was sure the auction was happening as scheduled and she informed him of its location.

Sparks looked at the oscilloscope that monitored Steel's vital signs. "Your respiration's still funky. Those broken ribs bothering you?" she asked.

They were, but Steel denied it. "Naaaaw."

Sparks mimicked him, sounding tough. "'Naaaaw. We can handle it. We're men.' I'm worried about you, Johnny." Her voice sounded concerned now. "Going in with less than—hang on, I got something."

Sparks interrupted her lecture to check a monitor displaying a map grid of L.A. "Head for Eagle Rock Boulevard. North of the river."

She worked the keyboard feverishly. Another monitor pulled up a satellite photo and zoomed in on it. "I'm scoping the image from LandSat. Looks like some kind of old factory."

Through her transceiver, she heard Uncle Joe gun the motor as the van turned onto the freeway following her instructions.

"Be right back. I'm calling in the cavalry," Sparks said.

She reached out and keyed a switch. Into her microphone, she said, "Strike Force David, this is—"

A man's hand reached down beside her and clicked the switch off, interrupting her transmission.

Startled, Sparks looked up into the barrel of a .45 pistol. One of Burke's mercenaries stared down at her with death in his eyes.

———

In the back of Joe's van, Steel spoke into his transceiver. "Sparky? Confirm that you've contacted David. Sparky . . .?"

Uncle Joe wrinkled his forehead. "Out of range?" he asked.

Behind his mask, Steel sounded worried. "Shouldn't be," he said. "We don't have much time. Better keep going."

Steel and Uncle Joe crouched in the storage yard near the abandoned mill complex. At first glance the mill, sitting on the L.A. River, looked deserted in the moonlight.

Then they noticed a tough-looking guard patrolling the perimeter with Dobermans on leashes, and a parking lot crowded with sleek limos and rugged all-terrain vehicles.

As Steel peered through the nightscope he had flipped up on his hammer, his armor flashed in the moonlight.

"I'm going in," he said. "If you can't raise Sparks, get to David through the satellite link."

"Be careful. You're not Superman. And you're not getting paid for this," Uncle Joe murmured. Then he turned quietly and hurried back toward the van.

Joe slipped along the road beside the storage yard toward the deep shadows where his truck was parked. He didn't notice that a guard was following him.

Steel moved stealthily toward the edge of the complex, then ducked back. The guard with the Dobermans was coming.

Steel adjusted the sonic switch on his hammer. It emitted a squeal too high for humans to hear.

The Dobermans whined and pawed their ears.

"What's the matter with you?" the guard snarled, as the big dogs dragged him away from Steel.

Steel climbed up a fire escape to a high mezzanine window and stepped quietly onto a catwalk. Looking down, he spotted a famous American underworld kingpin and a well-known Colombian drug lord among a large crowd of skinheads and mercenaries from around the world.

Then he crept farther out on the catwalk.

Before the assembled mass of paid cutthroats and criminals, Nathaniel Burke stood on a platform. His arms swept wide in a dramatic gesture as he displayed one of the pulse rifles Steel himself had helped to design.

I was right, Steel said to himself. It was Burke who had copied the weapons' designs, who had manufactured and distributed them, who was ultimately responsible for a recent string of robberies, injuries, and deaths. And who was now peddling these same weapons around the world.

Steel fought down a rush of intense fury. There was too much at stake to give in to his anger now. First, he needed information.

Perched high on his catwalk, Steel strained to hear what Burke was saying. He flipped a switch, and the hammerhead fanned out into a dish antenna that picked up Burke's voice.

"With the help of Mr. Daniels here, I've already made quite a few of these dandy little toys," Burke told his audience. "You've all seen these weapons at work on TV. Tonight I'm going to give you a live demonstration."

A voice behind Steel muttered, "Game's up."

Steel whipped around. The guard fired a sonic rifle right at Steel's chest. *Ka-vwoom!*

Steel flew backward over the catwalk, plummeted through the air, and landed hard on the platform, right in front of Burke and the startled criminals of the world. His hammer was jarred from his hand.

Burke's cold eyes looked into Steel's furious ones. "Took you long enough to get here, *Steel,*" he said.

Steel grabbed for his hammer. Burke put his foot on the shaft, blocking him. "Uh-uh-uhhh . . . you might want to think about that," he cautioned.

A door slid open, revealing an angry Sparks, helpless in her wheelchair. A guard had his gun pressed against her temple.

Steel was shocked. He knew that if he resisted, Burke would have Sparks killed without a second thought. He pulled his hand away from the hammer.

"See, that's the difference between us," Burke said, snatching up the hammer victoriously. "I'd kiss her sorry, wheelchair-bound butt good-bye and worry about myself."

Burke's lieutenant, Singer, stepped forward, pulse rifle in one hand, and jerked Steel to his feet. Burke resumed his sales pitch.

"Now, gentlemen, here's the deal. I can supply you with weapons like these on a sort of permanent lease."

Over the rumble of outrage that greeted this announcement, a skinhead shouted, "Lease? What the blazes are you talking about?"

Burke answered serenely. "These weapons are highly sophisticated electronic devices that require specialized maintenance and recharging. Only I will be able to do that for you."

Big Willy Daniels stepped forward, a proprietary grin on his face. "Only *we*!" he amended.

Burke pulled a pistol from his pocket, pointed it, and casually fired a burst of energy. Daniels flew backward and lay still. "Only *I*," Burke said coldly.

Even his hardened audience was stunned into momentary silence. Then the rumble of outrage began again. "That's blackmail!" the American kingpin shouted above the din.

Burke folded his arms, the pistol still in his hand. "No, it's just business," he replied.

"How much?" a voice with a Turkish accent shouted.

Burke smiled. "Millions. But, hey, I'm sure you all can afford it."

A mercenary was indignant. "You don't need our money. You can steal all you want."

"Oh, this isn't really about money," Burke chided him coldly.

An Australian called out, "You'll be the illegal arms supplier to the world. You want the power."

Burke smiled dangerously. Finally, they were getting it.

Steel and Sparks traded worried glances.

"Hey, I know it's a pain for you guys, but think about it," Burke said. "Do you really want to be the only one on your block without my kind of firepower when the rest of these nice folks start World War Three?"

Burke reached into his pocket and pressed the button on a remote control. A large door rumbled aside to reveal the dark Humvee. Slats, Holdecker, and their gang stood beside it, grinning and cocky.

"Before you answer that, let me give you that demonstration I promised," he continued. "You remember the stars of my little infomercial? My custom-designed

Humvee—the world's finest bankmobile—and the members of the Marks gang—who, incidentally, have served their purpose."

The gang's grins faded as Singer and another guard leveled pulse rifles at them. Slats glared at Burke. "What's this, man?" he asked.

Burke smiled. "I always use expendable rats for preliminary testing."

Singer casually fired a small static burst, which slammed Slats against the side of the Humvee. The rest of the gang gasped, horrified, wondering who would be next.

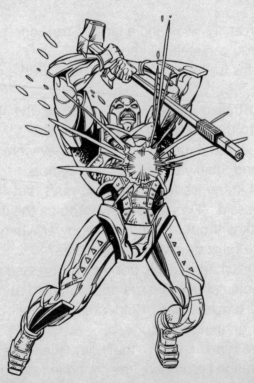

The Hammer
Does the Talking

Uncle Joe climbed into his van and keyed the radio. "Sparks? Do you read?"

There was no answer. "We're in real trouble," Joe muttered to Lillie, who lay panting in the back.

"You got that right. Step away from the truck, old man," a voice said from behind him.

Uncle Joe raised his hands and moved away from the door. The guard stepped between him and the truck, gesturing for Joe to head back toward the mill.

Suddenly, a furiously growling golden fury rocketed from the truck's window and pinned the guard to the ground.

Uncle Joe grabbed the guard's rifle. As Lillie growled threateningly, Uncle Joe tied the guard to a nearby tree and gagged him.

Then he stroked Lillie's soft golden head. "I owe you a steak, Lil," Joe said.

Inside the mill, Burke's auction was in turmoil. Daniels was dead, and Slats lay slumped against the Humvee, barely moving.

Burke held up his hand to quiet the meeting. "You've seen how powerful *these* weapons are . . . but, gentlemen, I've developed a new one five times more powerful! Wait till you—"

Steel's booming voice interrupted Burke. "Only five times more powerful? What've you got there, a water pistol? My hammer's got more juice than that," he scoffed.

Burke held up the hammer and sneered, "That's somewhat hard to believe."

Steel spoke to the assembled criminals. "I'll let my hammer speak for itself."

He looked at Burke. "See that slide on the right? Push it forward."

Warily, Burke pushed the slide forward, and the trigger popped out of the shaft.

Steel looked worried. "Just don't twist the red switch or she'll be too hot for you to handle."

Burke glanced sharply at Steel. "Really? You know, I was planning to use *you* to demonstrate the effectiveness of my new cannon. Killing two birds with one stone, as they say. But murdering you with your own hammer will be even more satisfying."

Burke laughed nastily as his finger curled around the

trigger. "And after you're gone, I'll still have Sparks for target practice!"

Two helicopters lifted off the LAPD helipad. The skyline glittered beyond them.

In the command chopper, Colonel David spoke into the radio to his anonymous informant. "We're airborne. Be there in fifteen."

From his van, Uncle Joe answered, "I hope you make it in time!"

He threw the microphone down on the seat and looked at Lillie in despair. "They aren't going to make it."

Inside the mill, Burke carefully studied the hammer. He looked at the tiny red switch. Then at Steel, who swallowed hard.

Steel spoke urgently to the criminals. "I'm telling you, if he kills me, you'll all lose out."

One of the mercenaries and the Turk stepped forward to protect him, but a guard waved his pulse rifle to stop them.

Burke raised the hammer to his shoulder. "We don't need you anymore. Except as a target."

He aimed the barrel at Steel, then paused, his eyes glinting. "Not the red switch, huh? Now, you know I just have to push the envelope."

He flipped the red switch.

"Yeah. I know you do." Steel grinned fiercely. Although he didn't realize it yet, Burke had just engaged the electromagnet.

Instantly, the hammer flew out of Burke's hands and slammed against Steel's armor. Burke was startled, then furious. "Kill him!" he roared.

"No way," Sparks shouted.

She hit a switch on her wheelchair and a laser beam speared out of the handgrip. It burned a dime-sized hole into the wall beyond the heads of the startled bidders. She hit a second switch and her wheelchair spun, sweeping the beam toward the guards, the gang, the criminals, and Burke. All dove for cover.

The criminals scrambled over each other to get out of the building.

Slats's gang fired conventional automatic rifles at the guards, who returned their fire with bursts of roiling energy, blasting the gang backward, shredding the walls with blistering cross fire.

Burke fired his pistol at Steel, but Steel ducked, and the energy burst blew out a window and slammed into the fuel tank of an ATV in the parking lot outside. With a shattering *ka-bloom!* the parking lot was transformed into an inferno.

The street gang's bullets ripped up the floor beside Burke. He ducked for safety as Steel leaped to protect Sparks with his armored body.

Behind his mask, John Henry's eyes crinkled. "Improvements on your chair?"

Sparks shrugged. "Give a girl a little free time and a couple of lasers, y'know?"

As roiling energy chewed up the wall beside them, Sparks returned the fire with a sonic blast from her chair. *Ka-vwoom!* The attacking guard flew backward right through a wooden wall.

Sparks smiled grimly. "Why should you have all the fun?"

Another fireball erupted through a wall. The inferno was spreading.

Steel could see Sparks had plenty of firepower. What she didn't have was armor. "Just get out of here quick!" he said. "I need you alive!"

Sparks's eyes glinted. "This quick enough?" she asked.

She hit another switch and a *whoosh!* of compressed air sent her chair zipping across the floor, upending Singer like a bowling pin on the way. Then she was out the door.

Steel gazed after her, amazed. Suddenly he heard Slats yell Burke's name.

Slats had staggered up and was firing at Burke, who returned his fire with a burst of energy. Slats crashed back into an industrial-strength circuit box, which exploded in a storm of sparks. Slats lit up like a neon sign, taking the mill lights out with him.

The complex was now lit by flames from the rapidly expanding fire. As Steel searched for Burke, he heard a shout for help.

Holdecker and three other gang members were out of ammunition and trapped by Singer. One teenager took a static energy burst and went down. Steel raised his hammer and fired a sonic blast, blowing an escape hole in the wall behind them. Steel yelled, "Get out! Run!"

They ran out through the hole in the wall, dragging their fallen comrade. Behind them, the mill was beginning to collapse. A burning beam crashed down in front of Singer, blocking his escape.

Steel turned to scan the burning building for Burke. He spotted him running toward the Humvee.

Leveling his hammer at the villain, he shouted, "Burke! Give it up!"

Burke dodged past the Humvee and toward an equipment closet. "First let's see what's behind door number two!" Burke yelled.

He wrenched open the door. Inside the closet was Martin, huddled and scared.

"My new best friend! Comfortable enough to come here on a field trip with ol' Mr. Large," Burke sneered. "Understand, Johnny? Success has never been enough for me. I need to see my enemies suffer."

Dragging Martin in front of him, he edged toward the Humvee. "Now, why don't you move so Martin and I can take a drive," he said threateningly.

"Guess again!" a solemn voice behind him said.

Burke wheeled around. Uncle Joe was leaning through a window, aiming the guard's pulse rifle at him.

In an instant, Burke fired. Uncle Joe flew backward, grabbing his shoulder.

Burke's hold on Martin had loosened, however, and the boy wrenched free. Enraged, Burke raised his pistol to fire after him.

Steel dove at Martin, sweeping him into his arms. He hit the ground hard and rolled through a door and into a burning side section of the mill.

Singer staggered to his feet just outside the door. He pulled the pin on a grenade, tossed it in after them, slammed the door, and bolted it. Steel and Martin were trapped!

24

Trapped

Martin looked around desperately. All the walls were on fire. "There's no way out!" he cried.

Steel grabbed the grenade. He spotted a small hole high over the door.

"Throw it! Quick!" Martin shouted.

Steel aimed, then paused. "I never make these."

"Bend your knees and follow through," Martin said. "Come on. You've gotta!"

Steel looked at Martin. He drew a breath. And lobbed the grenade.

It arced up and up and *swoosh!*—soared through the hole.

"Yessss!" Martin punched his fist in the air in a dance of victory.

Outside, Singer was counting down, anticipating

the explosion that would signal Steel's destruction. ". . . .three . . . two . . . one . . ." Suddenly the grenade bounced down beside him. His eyes went wide with horror.

Singer's terrified "Nooooo!" was drowned out by the roar of the explosion.

From outside the burning room, there was a resounding *bwoom!* as the door blew open.

Steel and Martin rushed out and looked around for Burke.

Up ahead, to one side of the burning platform, Burke was climbing into the Humvee. His eyes locked with Steel's. "Never saw my newest toy, did you, Steel?" he shouted. "Let's see how that armor of yours stands up to this!"

Burke keyed a switch. The roof of the Humvee whipped back, and a huge, futuristic cannon appeared, screaming as it charged.

"Steel, my friend, you're going to the scrap heap," Burke said, his eyes gleaming viciously. "Peace, John Henry. Or should I say *'pieces'*?"

Burke fired the cannon. A juggernaut of red electrical energy ripped like a gigantic buzz saw straight at Steel.

Steel turned his back, shielding Martin from the powerful burst. It smashed the armored giant full on the back, ramming him against Martin and the wall.

But his amazing armor did what it was designed to do. It reflected the red lightning storm right back to its source.

Burke was blasted through a support beam, and the blazing ceiling crashed down on top of him. He disappeared, screaming, into the conflagration.

Steel and Martin looked around. The huge building was engulfed in flames.

"We're trapped," Martin shouted. "There's fire all around us! How can we get out?"

Outside the burning mill, Sparks pulled the wounded Uncle Joe up onto her wheelchair. "Hang on!" she said.

She gunned her chair and sped toward the open tail-gate of the waiting van.

Behind her, there was a terrible roar. Looking back, she saw one side of the blazing mill explode outward. The Humvee blew in a spectacular arc through the fiery wall, coming right for Sparks and Uncle Joe.

Sparks desperately hit a button on her handgrip. There was the roar of a small jet engine, and her wheelchair rocketed forward, only seconds before the Humvee crashed to a landing where she and Uncle Joe had been just seconds earlier.

Inside the armored Humvee, Steel and Martin came to a stop. Martin was completely awestruck.

"Johnny? You're Johnny, aren't you?" he shouted excitedly. "You're the only guy I know who's as big as you but can't ever make a shot! Except this time you did! You said what you were making was top secret! And that armor's top secret! And the motorcycle, too!" He caught his breath, then added, "But mostly I know it's you 'cause of how you protected me."

Steel didn't argue. He shoved open the Humvee's door and spotted the van idling a short distance away. "Get in the van. Quick," he urged.

They scrambled up the back ramp. Sparks was behind the wheel, her wheelchair folded to one side. She hit a control and the ramp slammed shut.

Steel clambered forward and knelt beside Uncle Joe. Joe opened his eyes and grinned. "You did it, son!" he said. Steel smiled into his eyes. "You and Sparks—!"

Sparks kept her eyes on the road. But she pointed a finger at John Henry. "You!" she said.

He touched the tip of her finger with his own. "You!" he said back.

Uncle Joe chuckled. "Guess we did it together."

Martin was so juiced he couldn't stop babbling. "This is dope! My own brother is Steel! Yo, yo!" He turned to Steel, dead serious now. "I want to help you."

Steel opened his mouth to speak, but Martin was on a roll. "I could be like Robin! I could get a cape. We could be a team!"

Steel sighed. "Martin, do you want to know what you can do to help?"

His brother's eyes gleamed. "What?" he said. "I'll do anything!"

Steel closed his eyes. "Don't say *anything* about this to Grandma!"

The Best Part

Colonel David's troops rounded up the criminals who had fled the mill. Then the command chopper landed in the burning area, kicking up dust and flames. The colonel made his way over to where a soldier was giving first aid to one of Burke's guards.

"This one's willing to talk, sir," the soldier said.

The day was bright and filled with music. The neighborhood bustled. A group of kids was hanging out on a street corner.

"I heard Steel broke them fools off something ugly!" one kid said.

Another spoke in tones of awe. "He's like this giant, ten-foot, super robot! He kicks everybody's butt!"

"He's not a robot," an older teenager said. "He's a man. But he's more than that."

"Whatever. He needs to be sporting Marks' colors!"

"Don't talk that gang garbage," the older teenager snapped.

"What's up with you, Holdecker?" the younger kid puzzled. "You're a Mark, aren't you?"

"No more!" Holdecker said sternly. "There are no more Marks. That gang stuff's played out!"

Back in his office, Colonel David spoke genially into the phone, while nearby, a crisp lieutenant worked hurriedly to trace the call.

"Glad you called, Steel. The guard squealed. Fingered Burke. Coroner's still raking the rubble for his teeth. Guard also gave us another tape of the bank job. It showed a gang member shooting the chopper. You're cleared. So . . ."

The colonel looked at the lieutenant, who shook her head and whispered, "We don't have him yet, sir. Keep talking."

Colonel David continued, "So why don't you tell me who you are behind that mask?"

John Henry spoke into a computer mike, which made his voice sound deep and threatening. Sparks put her hand over her mouth to stifle her giggles, and Uncle Joe's eyes twinkled.

"Doesn't really matter, does it?" Steel said. "I've accomplished all I wanted. You won't see me anymore."

Colonel David was alarmed. "What? Hang on, we

might be able to do some good work together in the future. I'd even consider giving you access to that hot Humvee. You could—"

John Henry laughed. "Colonel, trying to trace this call is a waste of time. Your com-data person's going to think we're in . . ."

"Cincinnati," Sparks said, her eyes twinkling.

"Cincinnati," John Henry said.

The lieutenant happily waved a printout. "Got it, sir!" she said. "He's at a diner in Cincinnati! Shall I—"

Colonel David sighed. "Forget it, Nancy. That'll be all." He didn't try to hide his annoyance. "Listen, just tell me the truth. Is that you, Irons?"

John Henry smiled. "Can't talk anymore, Colonel. Phone might not be secure. I'll be in touch."

He hung up and grinned at Sparks, and she grinned back.

Suddenly the door section of the dome flew open. Martin entered dramatically, striking a suave James Bond pose.

"My name is Irons. Martin Irons," he said. "Man, this place is totally awesome!"

Uncle Joe scowled. "Well, don't just come in without—"

". . . checking I haven't been followed and stuff," Martin completed the thought. "I got all that covered, man."

"We're going to close it up anyway," John Henry said.

Martin was appalled. "Why? You're just getting started. You could get paid for doing this!"

"Uh, guys?" Sparks interrupted the approaching argument. "Grandma Odessa's expecting us."

Grandma Odessa's Black and Bleu Restaurant was so packed that additional tables had been set up on the sidewalk. She had a table on the side especially reserved for her family.

She saw them coming down the street: Joe, Martin, John Henry, and Sparks. She placed a dish covered by a napkin on the table.

Martin dove into his chair. "I'll have today's special, please," he said.

John Henry kissed his grandma on the cheek. "Maybe you should find out what it is first," he said.

Grandma Odessa announced proudly, "Lobster served out of the shell with a sweet potato cream sauce garnished with crisped okra."

Sparks chuckled. "Grandma Odessa, you are amazing!"

Odessa smiled. "I'll tell you what sounds amazing—all this stuff on the news about that Steel man. Mmmm, hmmm."

Uncle Joe raised an eyebrow. "What you think about him, Odessa?" he asked.

Grandma Odessa gave a proud, sideways glance at John Henry. "I think anybody'd be mighty honored to have him in their family," she said. "Now I got a surprise, my *pièce de résistance.*"

She pulled the napkin off the dish, unveiling her special creation. It rose high and golden from its gleaming white casserole.

John Henry smiled. "You finally made a hominy souffle!" They started to clap and hoot their appreciation.

Odessa waved them to be quiet. "It'll cave in!"

Uncle Joe smiled proudly at the souffle. "Ain't that something? What people can do when they put their minds to it."

John Henry knew what he was getting at. "Yes, sir. And it's amazing what you can do when you've got the right kind of help." He grinned at Sparks. "And I do love those wheelchair modifications."

There was a sparkle in Sparks's eyes. "Oh, you haven't seen the best part!"

She touched a switch. Her wheelchair whirred, then slowly straightened upward. It lifted and held her. She was standing now, tall enough to be face to face with the seated, laughing John Henry.

John Henry wrapped an arm around her. "I love it, girl!" he said.

Sparks flung her arms around his neck and smiled into his eyes. "So do I!" she said.

John Henry, Sparks, and the whole family laughed together. For them, the neighborhood was the cheeriest place in the radiant City of Angels, and the sky overhead seemed to hold a sunny promise for the days to come.

Epilogue

It Isn't Over

In the Intensive Care Unit of a private hospital in a small town along the L.A. River, a nurse and doctor stopped by the bed of a newly admitted burn patient.

"Said his name's Bill Whitaker," the nurse whispered. "Hikers found him along an arroyo in Eagle Rock. Said his sleeping bag caught fire. No family."

The doctor turned away. "Probably just as well. With all those burns, nobody'd recognize him, anyway."

The patient was swathed in bloody, oozing bandages. His breathing was shallow and wheezing. His one exposed, bloodshot eye strained to see the TV attached to the room's ceiling. Yes, that's Steel on the TV screen, he thought, staring at the image taken at the robbery.

The channel two news reporter said a group of international criminals had been arrested for attempting to purchase illegal weapons. The station also confirmed that the mysterious armored man known only as Steel was primarily responsible for foiling the criminals' plan.

The burn patient quivered with pain and hatred as he stared at the image on the screen, a tightly wound, psychotic glint in his eye. In a rasping whisper, he promised, "It isn't over, Irons. The war . . . is just . . . beginning."

About the Author

LOUISE SIMONSON was born in Atlanta, Georgia, but has lived in New York for many years.

Her first job in comics was for Warren Publishing, where she eventually became vice-president and senior editor.

She worked at Marvel Comics as an editor of numerous titles, including *Star Wars* and *The Uncanny X-Men*. She left her editorial position to pursue writing, her first love, and created the award-winning *Power Pack* series. Among other titles she wrote for Marvel are *X-Factor* (in which she co-created the character Apocalypse) and *The New Mutants* (in which she co-created Cable).

Since working for DC Comics, Simonson has written *Superman: The Man of Steel.* The character Steel was co-created by her with Jon Bogdanove in 1994 as part of the "Death of Superman" storyline and continues to appear in his own ongoing comic book series.

Recently, Simonson has written a number of books for younger readers, including *Superman: Doomsday & Beyond*, an adaptation of the "Death of Superman" storyline, and *I Hate Superman!* (which she doesn't!).

Simonson lives in upstate New York with her husband, Walter, who is also a comic book writer and artist, and two noisy little dogs.